Enid Blyton

ONE-A-DAY
CHRISTMAS
STORIES

Enid Blyton

ONE-A-DAY
CHRISTMAS
STORIES

Illustrations by Mark Beech

h Hodder

HODDER CHILDREN'S BOOKS

This collection first published in Great Britain in 2024 by Hodder & Stoughton

1 3 5 7 9 10 8 6 4 2

A CIP catalogue record for this book is available from the British Library.

ISBN 978 1 444 97474 4

Typeset in Caslon Twelve by Palimpsest Book Production Ltd, Falkirk, Stirlingshire

Printed and bound in Great Britain by Clays Ltd, Elcograf S.p.A

The paper and board used in this book are made from wood from responsible sources

Hodder Children's Books
An imprint of
Hachette Children's Group
Part of Hodder & Stoughton
Carmelite House
50 Victoria Embankment
London EC4Y 0DZ

An Hachette UK Company
www.hachette.co.uk
www.hachettechildrens.co.uk

Contents

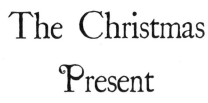

The Christmas
Present

The Christmas Present

'WHAT SHALL WE give Mummy for Christmas, Jinny?' said Johnny.

'I've seen something I *know* she would like,' said Jinny. 'It's in the jeweller's shop window. Come and see, Johnny.'

So Johnny went down to the village with Jinny, and she showed him what she had seen. It was a small brooch, and in the middle of it was the letter M in blue.

'There, M for Mummy,' said Jinny. 'Wouldn't you love to see Mummy wearing a brooch like that, that *we* gave her?'

'Yes. It would be nice,' said Johnny. 'I'm sure

Mummy would love it too. Then when people say to her, "Dear me, I didn't know your name was Margaret or Mollie or Mary," she can say, "It isn't! It's Mummy!'"

'It's five shillings,' said Jinny. 'That's a lot of money – especially as we have to buy presents for other people too.'

'We'd better try and earn some,' said Johnny. 'We'll ask Cook if she knows of a way we can earn money. We might chop wood or something.'

But Cook said nobody would let them chop wood. They would only chop their fingers instead. 'Now, I'll tell you what to do!' she said. 'You go down to old Mrs Kennet. She wants someone to do her shopping for her each day. She can't walk up and down the hill where she lives on these frosty, slippery mornings. I am sure she would give you a penny each errand.'

Well, Mrs Kennet was very pleased to see the twins, and delighted to think they would fetch her shopping for her.

'I can take my doll's pram to fetch it in,' said Jinny.

'And Johnny can take his barrow. Then we can bring quite a lot back for you, Mrs Kennet – potatoes and cabbages and all kinds of things. It will be fun.'

'It will be a good job of work,' said the old lady. 'Good work never hurt anyone – and good work should be paid for. I'm sure you are saving up to buy Christmas presents, aren't you? Well, I will pay you each tuppence every time you fetch my goods for me – that will be fourpence between you!'

'That won't be too much for you to pay, will it?' asked Jinny. 'We really meant to do it for only a penny a time.'

'Well, I'm paying you tuppence because of your having to come up this steep hill,' said Mrs Kennet. 'That's only fair. Now, you can begin today, if you like. The greengrocer has some carrots and onions for me, I want a loaf of brown bread, and a book from the library and a bag of flour.'

It was quite a lot of shopping to do. Jinny took her empty pram and Johnny took his little barrow. They got all the things that Mrs Kennet wanted, and then wheeled them up the hill to her house.

She was pleased. 'Here is your fourpence,' she said, and she gave two brown pennies to Jinny and two to Johnny. They ran home in glee and put them into their moneyboxes.

They told Mummy what they were doing for Mrs Kennet. Mummy said she thought they ought to help the old lady for nothing, but still, as they were saving up for Christmas, she was sure that Mrs Kennet was pleased to pay them.

'But you must do *some* of her errands for nothing,' said Mummy. 'Just to show her that you can be kind for no payment at all.'

So every third time they went on errands for Mrs Kennet the twins wouldn't take the pennies. 'We're doing your shopping today for nothing,' they told her. 'We want to.'

Each day they counted up their money for Mummy's Christmas present. And on the day before Christmas, what a wonderful thing – they had earned five shillings and fourpence between them!

'*Now* we can go and buy the brooch with M on,' said Jinny, and off they went.

They pushed open the door of the little jeweller's shop and went inside.

'Please can we have the brooch with M on?' asked Johnny, putting five shillings down on the counter. 'We want it for our mother.'

'Oh, dear – we sold it yesterday!' said the girl. 'I'm so sorry. It was the only one we had!'

The twins were dreadfully disappointed. They looked around the shop, trying to find something else that Mummy might like – but everything was so very, very dear. They hadn't nearly enough money!

They went out. Jinny's eyes were full of tears. 'Tomorrow's Christmas Day,' she said. 'And most of the shops have sold their nice things. We shan't be able to choose anything nice for Mummy now.'

Johnny had his little barrow with him, because Mrs

Kennet had asked him to bring back her turkey from the butcher's. 'We'd better take this turkey to Mrs Kennet,' he said. 'She said she was waiting for it. We might have time to run down to the village afterwards and find something for Mummy.'

They took the turkey in the barrow all the way up the hill. Mrs Kennet asked them in. 'I've got some chocolate buns for you,' she said. 'Dear me, what solemn faces! Whatever is the matter?'

'Oh, Mrs Kennet!' said Jinny. 'We've been working for you all this time, and saving up to buy Mummy a lovely brooch – and now it's sold. And it's too late to buy Mummy anything nice now. All the best things are gone.'

'Well, that's very sad,' said Mrs Kennet. 'But wait a minute – let me see now – I've some jewellery I am going to sell. Maybe I have a little brooch that your mother would like – one that I could give you, because you've been so very, very good to me.'

'That wouldn't do,' said Johnny. 'We've earned the money and we wanted to *spend* it on Mummy. It

8

wouldn't be the same if you just gave it to us for her. It wouldn't really be from us then.'

'Well, then, you may buy it from me, if you feel like that,' said Mrs Kennet, smiling. 'I'll fetch my jewellery case.'

She came back with a big leather box. She undid it – and, oh, what a lot of pretty things were there! Brooches, bracelets, necklaces, pins – but most of them were old and had lost their glitter and shine – and some were broken.

Suddenly Jinny gave a cry and pounced on a little brooch. 'Look! LOOK! Here's a brooch with M on it – and tiny little blue forget-me-nots all round it. It's much, much prettier than the one in the shop. Oh, Mrs Kennet, did one of your children give this to you years ago?'

'No,' said Mrs Kennet. 'It belonged to my aunt. Her name was Mary-Ann – and that's why the brooch has M on it. M for Mary-Ann. I was going to sell it – but if you like it, well, I will sell it to *you*! The letter M on it will do quite well for Mummy.'

'Is it very expensive?' asked Jinny. 'It's so very pretty, I'm afraid it will cost more money than we've got.'

'It's five shillings,' said Mrs Kennet, and the twins gave a shout of joy.

'We've got more than that! Can we clean the brooch and take it home with us? Here's the money, Mrs Kennet. Oh, it's a much, much nicer brooch than the other one!'

They cleaned the brooch, put it into a little box and took it home. They wrote a loving little message and put it on the breakfast table for Mummy the next morning.

'Oh!' she said, when she opened it. 'Twins! What a wonderful present! M for Mummy – and forget-me-nots all round it. Oh, it's my *nicest* present!'

'Yes, M for Mummy – and forget-me-nots to tell you we'll never, never forget you!' said Johnny, giving Mummy a hug. 'I'm *glad* you like it.'

Mummy did. She wears the brooch every single day. Wasn't it a wonderful Christmas present?

The Midnight
Goblins

The Midnight Goblins

THERE ONCE LIVED, many, many years ago, a poor shoemaker and his wife. The man worked very hard at making shoes, but somehow things went wrong for him. People did not pay their bills, his wife fell ill and had to have good food that took all his savings, and altogether the shoemaker was in a very bad way.

At last a day came when he had just enough money to buy the leather to make one more pair of shoes, and that was all.

He bought it and carefully cut out the shoes that evening.

'See, wife,' he said. 'This is my last pair of shoes. I

will sew them up tomorrow, and hope to sell them. If I do not, I cannot tell where the money for our next meal will come from.'

'Poor husband!' said the woman. 'You have worked so hard and so honestly. Surely good luck will come to us, even though this is the very last pair of shoes you have the money to make!'

The man put the cut-out shoes ready on a shelf, thinking to finish them early the next morning. Then he went to bed, and fell sound asleep.

Early next morning he got up, and drew the shutters back to let in the morning sun, so that he could see to finish the shoes. Then he saw something that made him stand still in the greatest astonishment.

There, on the shelf where he had put the cut-out leather the night before, lay a pair of beautiful little shoes! The shoemaker could hardly believe his eyes!

He stared and stared. Then he crossed over to the shelf and picked up the shoes.

'Marvel of marvels!' he cried. 'They are better made

than if I had made them myself! Every stitch is in the right place, and every nail neatly hammered home. This is indeed a mystery! Wife! Wife! What do you make of this?'

His wife was just as astonished as he was.

'It is magic, husband,' she said. 'But it is good magic, so put the shoes in the window and see if you can sell them.'

The man put the shoes in the empty window. Very soon a customer came by and was so pleased with the look of the lovely shoes that he offered the shoemaker twice as much as he expected to get. The cobbler was delighted, and ran in to tell his wife what good luck had come to him.

'There is enough money to buy bread for both of us, and leather for two more pairs of shoes,' said the shoemaker.

He went out to buy the bread, and brought home

some more leather. He cut out the two pairs of shoes and laid them on the shelf, ready to begin work early the next morning. Then he went to bed, and he and his wife slept soundly.

The next day he got up and took down the shutters as usual. He turned to look at his bench and – lo and behold! – there was his leather neatly made into two beautiful pairs of shoes again!

'There must surely be magic here!' said the cobbler, very much puzzled. He took the shoes up in his hands, and was delighted to see that they were just as well made as the pair the night before.

He put them in the window at once, and they had not been there five minutes before they were sold, for the passersby thought they looked so comfortable and so well made.

The shoemaker could hardly believe his good luck, for he was paid far more for them than ever he had been paid for shoes before.

'I shall buy meat for us, wife,' he said, 'and I will

buy you new ribbons for your bonnet. Even then I shall have enough money left over to pay for the leather for four more pairs of shoes!'

He went out and bought the meat and the ribbons. Out of the new leather he cut four pairs of shoes, and as usual put them up on the bench to finish early next morning.

When he pulled the shutters down he was not surprised to see the four pairs of shoes standing already made on the shelf, stitched as neatly as ever.

He had no difficulty in selling them for a very good price, and this time bought enough leather for eight pairs of shoes. Next morning they were all standing ready for him, and so it went on, night after night, and morning after morning. No matter how many dozens of shoes the shoemaker put out to finish in the morning, they were always ready for him, standing neatly in long rows on his bench. He sold them for a lot of money, and soon became very rich indeed, for the fame of his beautifully made shoes spread far and wide, and folk came from all over the place to buy them. Even the king at last sent for a dozen pairs, and then the shoemaker's fortune was indeed made, for everyone wanted to go to the same shoemaker as the king did.

Now Christmas time came near, and the shoemaker's wife began to wonder if they could do a good turn of some sort to the mysterious helpers.

'Husband,' she said, 'let us sit up tonight to try and find out who it is that comes to help us each night.'

'We will,' said the shoemaker.

So that night the shoemaker and his wife hid themselves behind a curtain in the shop. They left a lit candle on the table, so that they could see who came in, and then they waited patiently until the clock struck twelve.

Immediately the clock tolled twelve, the door of the shop flew open and in skipped two of the funniest little goblins ever seen. They were very tiny, and had hardly any clothes on, so they shivered and shook in the cold December night as they danced about the table and tried to keep themselves warm.

When they had finished dancing about they went to where the leather lay cut out on the bench, and sat down by it. They sat cross-legged just like the shoemaker did when he sat to make shoes. They threaded their needles and began to stitch. Stitch, stitch, stitch, they went, so fast that the shoemaker could not follow the thread with his eyes. Then they hammered away, and one by one the pairs of shoes were put on the bench, all neatly and prettily made. In the midst of their work the goblins began to shiver so much with the cold that they had to get up and jump about to warm themselves.

The shoemaker and his wife watched in wonder. They could hardly believe their eyes when they saw the shoes being made so quickly. Long before dawn they were all finished, and set out on the bench ready for the shoemaker to find in the morning. Then the goblins jumped down off the table and disappeared out of the door.

'Well, well, well!' cried the shoemaker, as soon as they had gone. 'Did you ever know such kind wee folk as those to come and help a poor man in his trouble like that? I do wish I could do something in return!'

'So you can,' said his wife. 'Did you notice how cold they were? The poor little things had hardly any clothes on! I will tell you what we can do. I will make them each a set of warm clothes, and you can make them a pair of tiny shoes!'

The shoemaker thought that was a very good idea. His wife bought some pieces of scarlet cloth and some lovely soft wool. Then she put on her thimble and began to sew little trousers as neatly as she could. She knitted two little coats as well, and very handsome they looked with tiny green buttons down each side. Then she knitted them the tiniest pair of stockings each, so small that they looked even too small for a doll.

The shoemaker was not idle. He made two pairs of red shoes, the tiniest ones that could be imagined, with little white buttons on each side. He was very proud of them when he had finished, for they were the daintiest and neatest things he had ever made.

When Christmas Eve came the shoemaker did not put the usual array of cut-out leather shoes on the bench for the goblins to finish, but put instead the two little suits, with the tiny red shoes on top. Then he and his wife hid themselves once more behind the curtain to see what would happen.

Exactly as the clock struck twelve, in hopped the two goblins as before, and skipped about to get themselves warm before sitting down to work.

Then they went to the bench to make the shoes. They were struck with astonishment when they saw the little scarlet suits of clothes waiting there for them! They picked them up with many little cries and calls of delight, and then began to dress themselves in them as fast as ever they could. When they came to the red stockings they screamed with joy, and as for the shoes, well, the goblins could hardly get them on, they were so pleased and excited!

When at last they were dressed they danced round and round the shop, singing and shouting for joy, and the shoemaker and his wife were delighted to see that the clothes and shoes fitted the goblins perfectly.

'Smart little goblins now are we,
Dressed in the finest of suits you see,
Never again will we shoemakers be!'

The goblins sang this song again and again as they danced about, and then suddenly rushed out into the night.

They never came back again after that to sew any more shoes for the shoemaker, but he was so rich that he needed no more help, and never lacked for money again.

But the curious thing was that every Christmas Eve after that the two goblins visited the shop to see if there were any new suits for them to replace the old ones that were beginning to wear out. And, of course, the shoemaker and his wife always put some ready, knowing that on Christmas morning they would find them gone.

The Christmas Tree Fairy

The Christmas Tree
Fairy

THERE WAS ONCE a hill which was covered with fir trees. They were fine trees, tall and straight, and always dressed in green, for they did not throw down their leaves in autumn as other trees did. They were evergreens.

'We must grow as tall as we can!' whispered the firs to one another. 'Tall, tall and straight.'

'I want to be the mast of a ship, then I shall always feel the wind rocking me,' said one fir.

'I want to be a telegraph post,' said another tree. 'Then all day and night I shall hear messages whispering along the wires!'

'I would like to be a scaffolding pole, put up when new houses are built,' said a third fir tree. 'I am so very, very tall.'

So the trees talked to one another – all but one small tree, which hadn't grown at all. The winter wind had once uprooted it, and it had nearly died. The woodman had replanted it, but it had never grown. It was a tiny tree, sad because it could no longer talk to its brothers.

They are so high above me that they would not even hear my voice! thought the little fir tree.

It was frightened when the woodman came round. It knew that the other trees were proud to know they would be masts of ships or something grand and useful – but what use would such a tiny tree be?

'One day I shall be chopped down, and made into firewood,' said the fir to itself. 'I am no use at all!'

And one morning, sure enough, the woodman came and saw the tiny tree. He didn't chop it down, but he dug it up. The little tree was sad. *Now, this is the end of me*, it thought.

To its great surprise, it was planted in a tub, which was painted bright red. And then all kinds of strange things happened to it!

The woodman's wife hung strands of tinsel on its boughs. She put bits of cotton wool here and there to make it look as if snow had fallen. She took bright shining glass balls and tied them to the dark little branches.

'The tree is looking lovely already!' she said. 'How pleased the children will be!'

Then she fastened twenty small and beautifully coloured candles, red, pink, yellow, blue and green, all over the tree. She tied a pretty fairy doll on to the top spike. She hung toys here and there. The tree was so astonished that it hardly knew what to think.

On Christmas Day the mother gave the little tree to her children. They clapped their hands in joy.

'Mother! Mother! It's a Christmas tree! Oh, Mother, it's the loveliest tree we've ever, ever had! Isn't it beautiful!'

The little fir tree was glad. It was happy to give pleasure to so many people. *Even if I am used for firewood now, I shan't mind!* it thought.

But after Christmas the woodman took the tree from its tub, and planted it in the garden round the cottage. 'It's just right for a Christmas tree!' he said. 'We'll have it for our Christmas tree every year!'

Wasn't that good luck for the little tree? I do hope you get one just like it for Christmas Day.

What They Did at Miss Brown's School

What They Did at Miss Brown's School

DECEMBER SLIPPED INTO the calendar and nobody noticed it, for the children were so busy making Christmas presents and seeing to their bird table that they did not realise November had gone.

But one day John said, 'Gracious! We break up next week – and we haven't done anything special for December, Miss Brown!'

'Well, you've been very busy indeed,' said Miss Brown. 'I hardly think you could have got anything else into our timetable, John.'

'But, Miss Brown, we can't leave December out. We

really *must* do something very extra-special as it's the Christmas month,' said Susan.

'Well, I hadn't forgotten, my dear,' said Miss Brown, laughing. 'But as the special thing I had planned for this month can come at the end of the term, I didn't say anything.'

'I suppose you thought we'd be so busy thinking of Christmas cakes and Christmas trees and presents that we would forget,' said Mary. 'What do you plan for us to do, Miss Brown? There's no snow, so we can't go out and find any snow tracks as we did in January. There's nothing to do in the garden, for we've dug it up, and burnt all our rubbish.'

'And our bulbs don't want much seeing to now,' said John. 'The Roman hyacinths and narcissi are flowering beautifully.'

'I wish we could give a treat to our friends, the birds,' said Susan, watching two tits swinging on the coconut by the window.

'Well, that's just what I thought we *would* do!' said

Miss Brown. 'We shall have Christmas cakes and Christmas trees – why can't we give the birds the same treat?'

'Oooh!' said the children, delighted. 'But how can we?'

'Do you mean *buy* a cake?' asked Peter.

'And would the birds *really* like a tree hung with toys and things?' asked Mary.

'Oh, we shall have to give them a special cake and a special sort of tree,' said Miss Brown. 'For one thing, we will make the cake ourselves, tomorrow morning. I will show you how to do it.'

Well, there was great excitement the next morning, as you can imagine! When the children came to school they saw that Miss Brown had put a big bowl on one of the tables, and around it were paper bags and tins.

'What's in the bags?' said Peter.

'Look and see,' said Miss Brown. So the children looked.

'Maize meal!' said Peter, shaking out a little into his

hand. 'And this bag is full of the hemp seeds we bought the other day. What are *these* seeds, Miss Brown – these little hard round seeds?'

'Those are *millet* seeds,' said Miss Brown. 'The birds love those – and in that next bag is the ordinary canary seed I give my canary. Now, will you please empty some of each bag into my bowl and mix up the seeds!'

That was a lovely thing to do. Eight hands at once mixed up the seed very thoroughly! Then Miss Brown made the children chop up brazil nuts and peanuts – all except Susan, that is, who always cut her fingers when she could, and was not allowed a sharp knife or pointed scissors. She was very upset until Miss Brown told her to go and fetch a bag of currants off the kitchen shelf and empty some into the mixed-up seed.

'Put the nuts into the bowl too,' said Miss Brown. 'That's right. Now we have maize seed, hemp seed, millet seed, canary seed, chopped-up peanuts and brazil nuts and currants in our mixture so far.'

'This will be a good cake!' said John, feeling quite hungry.

'Now I must get my melted fat,' said Miss Brown, going to the schoolroom fire, where a pan was sizzling with melting dripping. She poured the hot melted fat into the bowl, and let Mary stir it with a long spoon.

'Good!' she said. 'Our cake is finished!'

'But what about cooking it?' asked Mary, in surprise.

'It doesn't need to be cooked!' said Miss Brown. 'Look, I'll just get a cloth – here is one – and empty the whole mixture into it – and tie it up tightly like this – and then we'll put it in the larder and let it dry. Then we will cut slices out of it for the birds!'

'Oh, Miss Brown, I do think that's a good idea,' said Mary. 'I shall make a cake just like this at home. It's so easy!'

'Well, be careful of the boiling fat, if you do,' said Miss Brown. 'Here is the cake all tightly wrapped up in the cloth, Mary. Go and put it at the back of my larder on an enamel plate. Next week we will give the birds a slice of their Christmas cake each day.'

'We could put berries in the next one we make, couldn't we?' said Susan. 'Wouldn't the birds like yew berries and holly berries mixed in too?'

'Oh yes,' said Miss Brown. 'Sometimes I collect the autumn berries and dry them, and then use them for the bird cake too – but the one we have made will please the birds very much indeed.'

'And now, what about the Christmas tree?' asked John. 'I saw such a dear little tree at the greengrocer's yesterday, Miss Brown. It was ninepence.'

'That will do very well,' said Miss Brown. 'I will give you the ninepence, John, and you shall buy it for us and bring it to school yourself.'

Next morning John brought the tree along. It really was a nice little tree, with a big spike at the top. John put it into a big pot and made the earth firm around the roots.

'What are you going to hang on it?' asked Susan. 'Dolls and trains?'

Miss Brown laughed. 'No,' she said, 'I don't think the birds would enjoy those much – and nobody would be more surprised than you, Susan, if you saw a sparrow nursing a doll, or a blackbird driving a toy train.'

Susan giggled. 'Well, what *are* we going to hang on the tree?' she asked.

'Something for the birds to *eat*, of course,' said John. 'Bits of coconut would be good, wouldn't they, Miss Brown?'

'Very good,' said Miss Brown.

'And bits of bacon rind and a bone or two!' said Peter.

'And a few biscuits, perhaps!' said Mary.

'And what about threading strings of peanuts and hanging those here and there, or winding them about the branches!' cried John, getting excited.

'Oh yes – and we could spare a bit of mistletoe with berries on, for the mistle thrush!' cried Susan. 'He likes mistletoe berries, doesn't he, Miss Brown?'

'Very much,' said Miss Brown. 'And another thing

the birds love on a Christmas tree are two or three millet-seed sprays – we can buy them at tuppence each – big sprays of millet seeds on a long stalk!'

Well, it wasn't long before the children got to work on their Christmas tree for the birds. Miss Brown gave Mary sixpence to buy three millet sprays, and these were tied to the branches. They were full of little hard millet seeds, beloved by the sparrows and finches.

John bought a coconut from his own money. He cut the white nut into small pieces and tied each piece to the tree, so that they hung down like toys.

Mary brought some biscuits with little holes in. She threaded a piece of cotton through one of the middle holes and hung the biscuits on the tree too.

Peter brought two small bones and some bacon rind, which he tied carefully to the branches as well. The tree was really beginning to look very full.

Then all the children threaded a string of peanuts each, driving their big needles through the shells and stringing them together. The peanuts looked wonderful hanging down from the tree. And last of all, a spray of mistletoe was tied to the top spire.

'Now our tree is finished,' said Miss Brown. 'Doesn't it look fine! We will put it out for the birds before we break up, even though Christmas is not yet here, because it will be such fun to see them all enjoying it.'

So out went the tree in the middle of the lawn – and do you know, in two or three minutes the tits and the robin had found it and were having a lovely time in it! The robin perched right at the top and sang a little song, very short and sweet. The tits attacked the coconut and the peanuts and were delighted to see so much food in one place.

Then the sparrows flew down and pecked the biscuits, and the chaffinches discovered the millet seeds. A big blackbird decided he would like a biscuit, and two starlings squabbled over a bone. It really was fun to watch the tree so full of birds.

'Could we see if our cake is ready yet?' asked Susan. 'We could give the birds a piece if it is.'

Mary was sent to fetch in the cake, still tied up in its cloth. She undid it – and there was the bird cake, quite dry and ready to be eaten. It did look nice.

'You can cut the first piece, Mary,' said Miss Brown. So Mary proudly took a knife and cut a big slice of the cake. It did look lovely with all the currants, nuts and seeds inside!

'Please could I taste just a little tiny bit of it?' begged Susan.

'Of course not, Susan,' said Miss Brown. 'You know perfectly well that no food prepared for animals or birds should be eaten by children – why, just suppose we had put yew berries into this! They would poison you!'

'It does look so nice, though,' said Susan. 'Can I put it on the bird table, Miss Brown?'

Miss Brown said yes, so Susan put it there – and almost at once the birds found it. How they enjoyed it! They each found something they liked in it, and pecked away at the seeds, currants, nuts and fat for all they were worth. It was a very pleasant sight to see.

'Well, Miss Brown,' said Mary, as the children watched the birds, 'each month I've thought that we did something nicer than the last – but I *really* think this month has been the best!'

'Good!' said Miss Brown. 'Well, we've had a lovely year together – and if we've learnt to understand and to love the world around us more than we did a year ago, then we have done well!'

They really did have a lovely time, didn't they? Perhaps you will be able to share the same fun each month, then you will know how much the children at Miss Brown's school enjoyed it. And now we will wish them a very happy Christmas, and say goodbye until the next year.

The Stolen
Reindeer

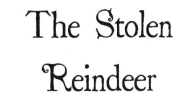

The Stolen Reindeer

SANTA CLAUS DROVE up to Toyland a week before Christmas.

'Whoa! Whoa!' he cried to his eight great reindeer as they arrived at the gates.

The gates slowly opened, and a crowd of gnomes and fairies rushed out.

'Welcome! Welcome! Santa Claus!' they cried, crowding round the big jolly man dressed in a red coat.

'Glad to see you all again!' beamed Santa Claus. 'Now, just get out of the way a bit, and let me drive my reindeer through the gates into Toyland!'

The crowd ran back, and Santa Claus drove straight

through the gates, which shut after him. With fairies and gnomes hanging on to his sledge he drove down the higgledy-piggledy streets of Toyland.

'Here we are!' he cried at last as he arrived in front of a large house, which looked really rather like a very smart doll's house. On the steps stood the mayor of Toyland, a little gnome, dressed in a flowing cloak of yellow.

'Welcome, Santa Claus!' called the mayor, going down the steps to greet his visitor, and nearly tumbling over his long cloak. 'We are very glad to see you here again. I hope all the orders you gave us for toys and games have been carried out in a satisfactory manner!'

'I hope so too,' answered Santa Claus, getting out of the sledge. 'I've got just a week to go round Toyland and collect all the toys before I start off on Christmas Eve to deliver them to the children!'

He went into the mayor's house and the mayor gave him an excellent dinner, for Santa Claus had driven many, many miles over the snow.

'Splendid!' said Santa Claus when he had finished.

'Now will you kindly give me the list of orders I sent you, and I will start on my journey round Toyland.'

The mayor took a very long piece of paper from a locked drawer and gave it to Santa Claus.

'Hmm, let me see. The blue fairies are dressing all the dolls this year. I must see if they are ready. The pink fairies are furnishing all the doll's houses. The water pixies are doing all the ships and boats; they ought to be well done this year!'

'I think you will find most of the things are ready for you to take,' said the mayor, looking over Santa Claus's shoulder.

'The gnomes are making the soldiers and forts,' went on Santa Claus, glancing down the paper, 'and the wise elf is looking after the book department and the games. What are the red goblins doing?'

'They are making boxes of crackers for the children to pull on Christmas Day, and when they have parties,' said the mayor. 'I haven't heard anything of them for some time, but I hope they are getting on all right.'

'Well, I'll visit the blue fairies first,' said Santa Claus, getting up from his armchair. 'I'll drive round in my sledge, and put the toys in as I go round for them.'

He jumped into his sledge, shook the reins and drove off to the blue fairies. They lived in the centre of Toyland, in a number of tiny little houses. When they heard his sleigh bells they rushed out.

'Hurray! Hurray!' they cried. 'Here's Santa Claus at last! Come and see all the dolls we've got!' And they dragged him laughingly into the middle house.

In the dining room were all sizes and shapes of dolls. They were sitting in chairs, standing up or leaning against the wall. Some were grown-up dolls, some were dressed like boys and girls, and all of them looked spick and span and beautiful.

'Excellent!' cried Santa Claus. 'You *have* worked hard. But where are the baby dolls? We *must* have baby dolls, you know!'

The blue fairies took him upstairs and there, cuddled in little beds, were the baby dolls, some in long clothes, and some in short baby dresses.

'Sh,' whispered the fairies, 'they're all asleep! Aren't they sweet?'

'They're lovely,' answered Santa Claus, 'and the children will love them, I know. But you can wake them up, and get all of them ready to go in my sledge for me! I want to take them now.'

'Oh, yes, certainly,' said the blue fairies, and they quickly gathered all the lovely dolls from downstairs and upstairs, and soon Santa Claus had them packed safely and comfortably in his big sledge.

'Goodbye!' he called to the fairies as his reindeer started off. 'Goodbye and thank you! You've done very well this year!'

Santa Claus then drove to the water pixies and they were so busy that they didn't hear him coming.

'Goodness me! They *are* busy!' said Santa Claus to

himself as he watched the pixies. They lived in a large blue lake on which were growing great white and yellow water lilies, and on the flat lily leaves were their houses.

The pixies were sailing a large fleet of ships, boats and steamers.

'Hi! Look out!' called a pixie. 'Your boat's going to bump into mine!' And he plunged into the water and twisted the boats in different directions.

'They sail beautifully!' cried another pixie. 'Won't the children be pleased with them!'

A tiny little pixie appeared at the door of a house, carrying a submarine.

'Look what I've just finished making!' he cried. 'See if it goes well in the water!' And he launched it from his lily leaf.

'Splendid! Splendid!' cried Santa Claus and all the pixies as they watched the submarine chugging through the water.

'Here's Santa Claus! Hurray!' shouted the pixies, scrambling out of the water to greet him.

'Your boats are fine!' said Santa Claus, smiling. 'Are they ready to be packed into my sledge?'

'Yes, we've just finished them all!' said the pixies, swimming after the floating fleet of ships.

'I'm very pleased with you,' beamed Santa Claus, when the ships were all neatly packed in the sledge. 'I'm going off to the wise elf now for books and games. Goodbye!' And off he went.

The wise elf was very pleased to see Santa, and told him all the books were ready and all the games as well. The elves soon brought out great parcels of them, and they too were packed in the sledge.

'Thank you,' said Santa, taking up the reins. 'Now I'm going back to the mayor, to sleep at his house for the night.'

The next day Santa Claus drove off to the pink fairies to get the doll's houses, and he was very pleased indeed with them.

'We've hung up frilly curtains in all the windows,' said the little fairies, 'and we've put down carpets to match the wallpapers in every room, and we've made all the sheets and blankets for the beds and polished up everything we could.'

Santa Claus peeped into one or two doll's houses.

'They're quite perfect,' he said, 'and I am awfully pleased. Pack them at the back of my sledge please. There's room there.'

It took such a long time to pack them in properly that Santa had no time to do anything more that day, except drive straight to the mayor's.

He took three days seeing over the forts that the gnomes had made, and there were so many thousands of soldiers to look at that Santa Claus thought he would never come to the end.

'You've worked really splendidly,' he said to the busy little gnomes. 'Now put them in my sledge quickly. I've only one day left to collect the boxes of crackers from the red goblins, and then I must start on my travels for Christmas Eve.'

The next day he started off for the caves where the

red goblins lived. He left his sledge and reindeer outside the caves and strode into them. Not a single sound could he hear.

'Bless me! They're all asleep!' exclaimed Santa Claus in great astonishment.

Sure enough they were! They lay all around the middle cave, snoring.

'Wake up! Wake up! You lazy little creatures!' cried Santa, clapping his hands.

The red goblins sat up.

'Oh! Oh! Oh!' they cried. 'Here's Santa Claus, and we haven't finished our work!'

'Not finished your work!' thundered Santa Claus, frowning. 'What in the world do you mean!'

'Please, we didn't have enough gunpowder to put in the crackers, so we couldn't make enough!' explained a goblin, trembling.

'You *did* have enough; you had more than enough! I sent you the gunpowder myself!' roared Santa Claus. 'What have you done with it?'

'Please don't be so angry with us!' begged the goblins. 'You see we had a big party on November 5th, and we used some of the gunpowder to make fireworks with!'

'Then you're very, very naughty,' said Santa Claus, 'and I shall punish you. Put the crackers you have made into my sledge at once, and come to the mayor's house after Christmas, and I will tell you what your punishment is to be!'

The goblins scurried about and Santa Claus scolded them. They were very sulky and sullen and glared at him whenever he spoke.

At last he went outside to get into his sledge. But it wasn't there!

'Where are my reindeer?' shouted Santa Claus.

'He, he! Ha, ha! Ho, ho!' laughed the wicked red goblins. 'You were cross with us, and now our two chief goblins have driven your sledge away, and you won't have any toys for Christmas!'

Santa Claus was in a terrible state of mind. He rushed into a shop nearby and bought a toy motorcar.

This will catch them up perhaps! he thought desperately. He wound up the motorcar, jumped in and started off. He saw the track of the reindeer on the road, and followed it as quickly as ever the toy motorcar could go.

On and on and on he went, swishing round corners, sounding his horn continuously.

Suddenly, far away in front of him, he heard the sound of sleigh bells.

'Hurray! I shall catch them before long!' yelled Santa. But just at that moment the toy motorcar stopped, and he had to get out and wind the clockwork up again. By that time he could hear the sleigh bells no more.

Presently it became dark, but still Santa Claus drove on and on and on, always listening for the tinkling sleigh bells.

All through the night he drove, until the day dawned.

'Goodness me! I'm right out of Toyland! I'm in the

country of the North Wind!' exclaimed Santa as he looked around, and got out to wind up his motorcar again. 'And, oh! Thank goodness, there's my sledge not very far in front of me!'

Santa Claus drove furiously, and at last caught up to the sledge! He blew a silver whistle that he had hanging round his neck, and at once the reindeer stopped, in spite of the two red goblins who were trying to make them go on.

Santa got out of the motorcar, and at the same moment the North Wind came up to see what the disturbance was.

'I give you these two red goblins as your prisoners,' said Santa Claus sternly. 'They have driven off with my sledge of toys, and tomorrow is Christmas Day! I shall only just have time to get to the world of boys and girls by evening now.'

'I'll keep them safely!' said the North Wind, grabbing hold of the wicked goblins and shaking them.

'Gee up! Gee up!' called Santa Claus to his reindeer.

But, alas! They had no sooner gone forward a step or two than all the reindeer fell down, gasping.

'Oh, dear, dear, dear!' cried poor Santa Claus in despair. 'Whatever *shall* I do! I *must* get the toys to the children somehow!'

'Take them in the toy motorcar,' suggested the North Wind.

'It's *much* too small,' said Santa Claus sadly.

'Oh, I can soon alter *that*,' laughed the North Wind. 'And as you've given me two prisoners to keep as servants, I'll be very pleased to!'

He suddenly pursed up his mouth and blew towards the toy motorcar three times. Immediately it grew to a tremendous size.

'Goodness!' gasped Santa Claus. 'That's splendid! Now then, you two goblins, I'll give you just half an hour to unpack all the toys out of the sledge and pack them in the motorcar!'

The two frightened goblins set to work, and soon all the toys were neatly packed into the car.

'Now I'm off!' said Santa Claus, getting into the car and taking hold of the steering wheel. 'Don't bother about my reindeer, they'll go back to their stables by themselves when they feel better. Goodbye!' And off drove Santa Claus as fast as ever the car would go!

And that Christmas night no child heard the sound of sleigh bells as Santa Claus went on his rounds.

'But I heard the sound of a great motor,' said one little boy to his mother. 'And when I looked out of the window to see why, there was a great motorcar full of toys, and Santa Claus was driving it!'

'Nonsense!' said his mother, smiling. 'You must have dreamt it! Santa Claus never uses a motorcar!'

But he did that year, and if that Christmas Eve *you* were awakened by the sound of a motor in the middle of the night, you will know what it was – it was the toy motorcar Santa Claus had to use when the red goblins ran away with his reindeer!

The Vanishing
Nuts

The Vanishing
Nuts

IN THE GARDEN belonging to Apple Tree Cottage there were twenty-two nut-trees. Susan, George and Peter's great-grandfather had planted them, because he had been very fond of nuts – and now they had grown into fine trees that bore heaps of big nuts every year.

Susan, George and Peter were very fond of nuts too. They helped to pick them and in return they were given a big dishful for themselves. They helped to pack up boxes of nuts too, to send away to their father's brother and sisters. Nut-time was a very busy time indeed!

Father always used to put aside a boxful of the very finest nuts for Christmas time. He carried it up into the attic room, and popped it on the floor there. Then, at Christmas, the box was taken downstairs and the nuts were set out in pretty little dishes.

One autumn the nut-trees grew the biggest nuts they had had for years. Father was very pleased. He chose some fine ones to store away for Christmas, and George helped him to carry the box upstairs to the attic.

'Now, none of you children are to go to the attic for nuts,' said Father. 'But you all know that, very well, don't you?'

'Yes, Daddy,' said Susan, George and Peter. 'We promise we won't.'

Father didn't think any more about the Christmas nuts until one day when he happened to go upstairs to fetch a pair of old boots from the attic. He happened to glance at the box of nuts – and then he stood still and frowned.

'Someone's been taking those nuts,' he said. 'Now, whoever can it be?' He went downstairs and found Mother.

'Have you taken any of the Christmas nuts from the attic?' he asked.

'No, dear,' said Mother in surprise. 'Why?'

'Because quite a number have gone,' said Father, frowning. 'Is it the children, do you think?'

'Oh, I hope not,' said Mother, looking worried. 'I don't think they'd take anything without asking. Do you?'

'Call them in here and I'll ask them,' said Father. So Mother called all the children, who were out in the garden, and the three of them soon came in and trooped into their father's study.

'Have any of you been taking the nuts from the attic?' said Father. 'Have you, Susan?'

'Oh, no,' said Susan. 'Of course not, Father.'

'What about you, George?' asked Father.

'I haven't either,' said George.

'Have you, Peter?' said Father.

'No, I haven't,' answered Peter. 'Why, Father? Have the nuts gone?'

'A good many of them have,' said Father. 'Well, you

may go. Remember never to take anything without asking, won't you?'

'Oh, yes, Daddy,' said all the children, and off they went. But they were very worried, because they couldn't bear to think that their father should even dream that they could take the nuts without asking him first.

'Whoever can it be?' said Peter. 'The baby-sitter hates nuts, so it can't be her.'

'And the cleaning lady's been away ill for a month, so it can't be her!' said George.

'Well, that only leaves us three and Mummy and Daddy!' said Susan, puzzled. 'Who on earth can it be?'

'We'll just wait and see if any more go,' said Peter. 'Then, if they do, we'll have to do something about it!'

The next week, Father went up to the attic again, to look at the nuts – and dear me, a whole lot more had vanished! How puzzled and grieved he was! He felt certain that it must be one of the children.

But each of them said, 'No, Daddy,' when he asked them.

'Well, it must be one of you,' said Father sadly. 'It can't be anyone else. It grieves me very much, children, for I didn't think any of you would do such a silly thing.'

Susan went out of the room crying, for she loved her father. George and Peter went very red, and when they were in the playroom they put their arms round Susan and hugged her and told her not to mind.

'It's not us, we know that,' said George. 'But it looks as if it quite easily might be us, so we can't blame Daddy for asking. The thing to do is to show him that it isn't us. Let's ask him to lock the door.'

So they went to ask Father. 'Very well,' he said, and he locked the door and put the key in his pocket.

But still the nuts vanished! Father became more puzzled than ever. He simply couldn't make it out.

'Anyway, that proves it isn't us,' said George, and Father smiled and said yes, it did, and he was very pleased indeed.

'I think it must be the fairies,' said Susan. 'Daddy,

will you let us hide in the attic cupboard and watch one night?'

'No,' said Father, laughing. 'If you want to do any watching, you must do it in the daytime.'

'But the fairies wouldn't come then,' said Susan. But Father wouldn't agree to night-time watching, so Susan decided to watch in the daytime.

That afternoon the three children climbed the stairs to the attic, feeling rather excited. They were quite determined to catch the thief.

They went to the cupboard and settled themselves behind the curtains. For a long time nothing happened. Susan began to feel sleepy – but suddenly George poked her in the back.

'Sh! Sh!' he said. 'Do you hear something?'

Susan and Peter listened. Yes! There was a little scraping noise that was coming from somewhere. Then there was a bump and a slither, and a patter across the floor!

Was it the fairies? How the children's hearts beat!

They peeped through the curtains, and watched the box of nuts. And then they saw the thief!

Who do you think it was? Why, it was a little squirrel who lived in the pinewoods nearby! The pretty creature had climbed up a tree by the attic window, jumped to the top of the open window, leapt down, and come to the store of nuts every day!

'Oh!' said Susan. 'So that's the thief! The cheeky little fellow!'

The squirrel heard the children in the cupboard, and pricked up his ears. Suddenly George rushed out from behind the curtains and shut the window with a bang. The door was already shut, so the squirrel was fairly caught!

'Let's fetch Daddy!' said Susan. 'Then he'll see who the thief is!'

So George opened the door a little way, and shouted 'Daddy! Mummy! Do come up to the attic! We've caught the thief!'

The children's parents came running up and slipped in through the door.

'There!' said Susan, pointing to the squirrel. 'What do you think of our thief, Daddy?'

'Well, well, well!' said Father in astonishment. 'A squirrel! Whoever would have thought it! He must have discovered our nuts and thought what a fine treasure-store he had found! Open the window and let him go, Peter.'

When the window was opened the squirrel hopped out and disappeared down the tree.

'The mystery is solved,' said Mother, 'and a good thing too! Come along downstairs, children, and I will give you cherry cake for tea as a reward for your discovery!'

'Hurrah!' shouted the children, and off they rushed downstairs!

The Christmas Tree
Aeroplane

The Christmas Tree Aeroplane

ALL THE CHILDREN in the village were as excited as could be, because the lady at the Big House was giving a party – and every boy and girl was invited!

'I'm going to wear my new suit!' said Alan.

'I'm going to have on my new blue dress,' said Eileen.

'There's going to be crackers and balloons!' said John.

'And an *enormous* Christmas tree that nearly reaches the ceiling!' said Harry.

'And a lovely tea with jellies and chocolate cake!' said Belinda.

'It will be the loveliest party that ever was!' said Kenneth.

'Look! There's the tree going up to the Big House!' cried Fred. All the children ran into the lane and watched the cart going up the snowy road, with a big Christmas tree lying on it.

'There's a fine pack of toys for this tree!' called the driver, who was Alan's father. 'I've seen them. My, you'll be lucky children!'

'What's for the top of the tree?' asked Belinda. 'Will there be a fairy doll?'

'No, not this year,' said the driver. 'There is something different – it's Santa Claus in an aeroplane! He's going to be at the top of the tree, looking mighty grand in his plane, I can tell you!'

'How lovely!' cried all the children – and they thought that it would be even nicer to have Santa Claus in an aeroplane at the top of the Christmas tree than a fairy doll.

At last the great day came. Everybody was

dressed in their best. Every girl wore new ribbons and every boy had brushed his hair down flat till it shone. They all went up to the Big House as happy as could be.

At least, all of them except Harry. He went with the others, but he didn't feel very happy. His suit wasn't new – it was only his old one, because he hadn't a best one. His shoes wanted mending, and he hadn't even got a clean hanky, because his mother was ill in bed and couldn't see to him properly. But Harry had washed his face and hands, and brushed his hair as well as he possibly could.

He soon forgot about his old suit and his old shoes. The children shouted with joy when they went into the big hall and saw the Christmas tree there. Its candles were not yet lit, but all the ornaments and presents hung on it, and it looked beautiful.

'Look! There's the aeroplane at the top of the tree!' cried Kenneth. Everyone looked – and, dear me, it certainly was a very fine aeroplane. It shone and glittered, and the little Santa Claus inside grinned in a jolly way at all the children.

'I wonder who will have the aeroplane for a present,' said John.

Mrs Lee, the lady who was giving the party, smiled at him. 'Nobody will have the aeroplane,' she said. 'I bought it to go at the top of the tree, not for a present. It is just to make the tree look pretty.'

The party was lovely. There were games of all kinds and there were prizes for those who won the games. Everybody won one except Harry, who really was very unlucky.

Then balloons were given out. Harry got a great big blue one. He was very proud of it. And just as he was throwing it up into the air, playing with it, he heard someone's balloon go pop!

It was little Janey's! She had thrown it by mistake against a spray of prickly holly, and it had burst. Janey burst too – into tears! She sobbed and sobbed – but there was no balloon left for her to have another.

Harry went up to her. 'Have my balloon, Janey,' he said. 'Here it is. It's a beauty. You have it, and then you won't cry any more.'

Janey was simply delighted. She took the blue balloon and smiled through her tears. 'Oh, thank you, Harry,' she said. 'I do love it!'

Wasn't it nice of Harry? He watched Janey playing with his balloon until teatime – and then the children sat down to a lovely tea. Oh, the cakes there were! And the dishes of jellies and blancmanges! They really did enjoy themselves!

At the end of tea, Mrs Lee gave each child three crackers. They pulled them with a loud pop-pop-pop! Out came toys and hats.

Harry was unlucky with his crackers. The other children who pulled with him got the toys out of his crackers – and he only got a hat. And that was a bonnet, so he gave it to Ruth.

The next exciting thing that happened was the Christmas tree! All the children went into the hall, and there was the tree lit up from top to bottom with pink, yellow, blue, green and red candles. It looked like a magic tree.

'Isn't it lovely!' cried all the children. 'Oh, isn't it lovely!'

Then Mrs Lee began to cut the presents off. As she did so, she called out a child's name.

'Kenneth!' And up went Kenneth and took a train.

'Belinda!' And up went Belinda and was handed a beautiful doll.

'Alan!' Up went Alan and had a big fat book of stories. It was so exciting.

But one little boy was left out! It wasn't Harry – he had a ship. It was Paul. For some reason he had been forgotten, and there was no present for him at all. Mrs Lee smiled at all the children and told them to go into the dining room again to play some more games – and Paul didn't like to say he had had no present from the tree.

'Where's your present, Paul?' asked Harry, as they went into the big dining room.

'I didn't get one,' said Paul, trying to look as if he didn't mind. 'Perhaps Mrs Lee doesn't like me. I was rather naughty last week, and she may have heard of it.'

'But, Paul, aren't you unhappy because you haven't got anything?' said Harry, who thought Paul was being very brave about it.

'Yes,' said Paul, and he turned away so that Harry shouldn't see how near to crying he was. It was so dreadful to be left out like that.

Harry thought it was dreadful too. He put his arm round Paul. 'Take my ship,' he said. 'I've got one at home. I don't need this, Paul.'

Paul turned round, his face shining. 'Have you really got a ship at home, Harry?' he said. 'Are you sure you don't want it?'

Harry *did* want it – but he saw that Paul wanted it badly too. So the kind-hearted boy pushed his precious ship into Paul's hands, and then went to join in a game.

When half past six came, the party was over. Mothers

and fathers had come to fetch their children. How they cried out in surprise when they saw the balloons, the cracker toys, and the lovely presents and prizes that their children had!

Only Harry had none. His mother did not come to fetch him because she was ill. His father was looking after her, so Harry was to walk the long dark way home by himself. It was snowing, so the little boy turned up his collar.

He went to say goodbye and thank you to Mrs Lee. He had good manners, and he knew that at the end of a party or a treat every child should say thank you very much.

'Goodbye, Mrs Lee, and thank you very much for asking me to your nice party,' said Harry politely.

'I'm glad you enjoyed it,' said Mrs Lee, shaking hands with him. 'But wait a minute – you have forgotten your things. Where is your balloon? And your cracker toys – and your present? You surely don't want to leave them behind.'

Harry went red. He didn't know what to say. But little Janey called out loudly, 'Oh, Mrs Lee, my balloon burst, so Harry gave me his lovely blue one. Here it is!'

'And he only got a bonnet out of one of his crackers,' said Ruth, holding up the red bonnet. 'So he gave it to me.'

'But where is your present?' asked Mrs Lee. 'I know I gave you a ship!'

'Here's the ship!' said Paul, holding it up. 'He gave it to me.'

'But why did you do that, Harry?' asked Mrs Lee in surprise. 'Didn't you like it?'

'I loved it,' said Harry, going redder and redder. 'But you see, Mrs Lee, Paul didn't get a present. You forgot him. And he really was very brave about it, so I gave him the ship.'

'Well!' said Mrs Lee in astonishment. 'I think you must be the most generous boy I've ever known. But I *can't* let you go away from my party without *some*thing! Wait a minute and let me see if there is anything left.'

She looked in the balloon box. No balloons. She looked in the cracker boxes. No crackers! She looked on the tree – not a present was left! Only the ornaments were there, shining and glittering.

'Dear me, there doesn't seem to be anything left at all,' said Mrs Lee. And then she caught sight of the beautiful shining aeroplane at the top, with Santa Claus smiling inside. 'Of course! There's that! I didn't mean anyone to have it, because it is such a beauty and I wanted it for the next time we had the tree – but you shall have it, Harry, because you deserve it!'

And she got a chair, cut down the lovely aeroplane, and gave it to Harry. He was so excited that he could hardly say thank you. He had got the loveliest thing of all!

The other children crowded round him to see. 'Oooh! Isn't it lovely!' they said. 'How it shines! And isn't Santa Claus real? You *are* lucky, Harry – but you deserve it.'

'Yes, he deserves it,' said Mrs Lee, smiling. 'And I am going to take him home in my car, because I don't want him to be lost in the snow. Wait for me, Harry!'

So Harry waited, hugging his fine aeroplane and feeling happier than he had ever been in his life. And when Mrs Lee came up with her coat on, she carried a box of cakes and a big dish of fruit jelly for Harry's mother.

'I thought I was going home with nothing – and I'm going home with more than anybody else,' said Harry in delight.

'A kind heart always brings its own reward,' said Mrs Lee. 'Remember that, Harry!'

He always does remember it – and we will too, won't we?

A Christmas
Story

A Christmas Story

IT WAS CHRISTMAS Eve. Mother was putting Jack and Peggy to bed, and they were hanging up their stockings.

'Are you going to hang up *your* stocking and Daddy's, Mother?' asked Jack. 'You want such a lot of things, don't you? I wish I had the money to buy you them! I would get you a new watch and a nice scarf for your neck. And I would get Daddy the best chocolate in the world and a pocketbook full of money.'

'Would you, dear!' said Mother. 'Well, it's kind of you to think of it – but I'm afraid Daddy and I will have to have empty stockings, because Father Christmas doesn't pay any attention to the stockings of grown-ups – he only fills those of children. Now go to sleep.'

The children snuggled down, and although they really were *very* much excited they did fall asleep at last – but they both woke up at midnight. Jack sat up in bed and listened.

'Peggy!' he whispered. 'Hark! Can you hear that funny noise downstairs!'

They listened. It sounded like someone groaning and grunting. They slipped on their dressing gowns and crept downstairs to the dining room, where the noise was coming from. And whatever do you think they saw? I'll give you three guesses!

They saw a pair of legs with big black Wellington boots on sticking out of the chimney! The legs were struggling wildly, and up the chimney was a noise of grunting and groaning. 'I can't get down,' said the voice, 'and I can't get up! I'm stuck! Whatever shall I do?'

'It's Father Christmas!' said Jack in great surprise

and delight. 'Come on, Peggy – take hold of a leg and pull him down the chimney! He's stuck!'

They tugged at the big legs – and, dear me, down the chimney came Father Christmas with a rush and sat heavily on the fender. He looked at the two children and laughed.

'I came down the wrong chimney,' he said. 'What a mercy you heard me! I might have stayed there all night! Thank you so much for your help! Now you shall choose two extra presents each for getting me out of my fix.'

He opened the neck of his bulging sack – and, my goodness me, what a crowd of wonderful toys he had. But Jack didn't want toys.

'Father Christmas,' he said, '*please* will you put the presents into Daddy's and Mother's stockings instead? I'd like a watch and a scarf for Mother and chocolate and a pocketbook of money for Daddy.'

'Of course I will!' said Father Christmas. 'I'm delighted to meet a child who doesn't think of himself. Fetch me the stockings.'

Off went Jack and Peggy and came back with a long stocking of their mother's and a great big one of Daddy's. Then into each of them Father Christmas stuffed the presents Jack had asked for, and the children hung them up at the end of Mother's bed.

And what *do* you think their mother and Daddy said when they woke up on Christmas morning and found that their stockings were full after all?

The Little
Fairy Doll

The Little Fairy Doll

IN THE TOY shop on a high shelf sat a little fairy doll. She was very, very small, only three inches high, but she was beautifully dressed in silver gauze and her wings were like a butterfly's.

All the other toys laughed at her because she was so tiny.

'Look at me,' said a big walking, talking doll. '*I'm* the sort of doll children like.'

'And look at me,' said a big teddy bear, pressing himself in the middle and growling loudly. 'Children simply love *me*. I'm a comfortable armful, I am.'

'And look at *me*,' said a sailor doll turning head-over-heels. 'I'm a fine big fellow, with hair so thick you could use it for a brush! You're no use at all, fairy doll! Who wants a creature as little as you? You're too small for a Christmas tree and too tiny to cuddle.'

The fairy doll was very unhappy. She badly wanted to go where there were children – but nobody came to buy her. She was so *much* too small. The sailor doll was bought, and the teddy bear, and the walking, talking doll went very quickly. But the fairy doll sat up on the shelf all alone.

Even the shopkeeper laughed at her.

'I shall never sell *you*!' she said. 'You're so tiny! You're of no use to anyone.'

Christmas Eve came and still the little doll sat up on the shelf, getting rather dusty now. She was very sorrowful, for she thought she would have a lonely Christmas. And then, just five minutes before the shopwoman shut the shop the door opened and the bell rang. In came a nurse and went to the counter.

'Have you anything to put on a children's Christmas cake?' she asked.

'I haven't anything at all,' said the shopwoman, looking round. 'I've sold every one of my cake ornaments.'

'Oh, dear,' said the nurse, looking worried. 'Whatever shall I do? There will be nine children to tea on Christmas Day, and our cake won't have any decoration! But look! What's that up on the shelf?'

'That?' said the shopwoman. 'Oh, that's a little fairy doll, not a cake ornament.'

'But she will do beautifully,' said the nurse excitedly. 'Why, she's just the right size! Get her down, will you? Oh, isn't she a little beauty!'

So the fairy doll was put on the Christmas cake, and the next day you should have seen her on the tea table! She stood in the very middle of the icing, with pink roses all round her, one leg stretched out and her wand held in front of her.

'Look!' cried all the children, crowding round.

'Isn't she lovely!' And they brought all their toys to see her. The sailor dolls, bears, bunnies and dolls all looked enviously at the little fairy doll and wished they were on the cake too.

When the cake was eaten the fairy doll was put right in the very middle of the nursery mantelpiece – and there she is still if you would like to see her!

The Very Lovely
Pattern

The Very Lovely Pattern

BETTY WAS SITTING in her seat at school, trying very hard to think of a lovely pattern to draw and colour.

'I'm no good at drawing,' said Betty to herself. 'Not a bit of good! I never shall be. But oh, I do wish I could think of a pattern to draw on this page, so that Miss Brown would be pleased with me!'

'Betty! Are you dreaming as usual?' said Miss Brown. 'Do get on with your work.'

'I'm trying to think of a pattern,' said Betty. 'But it's very hard.'

'No, it isn't. It's easy,' said Harry. 'Look, Betty – do

you see my pattern? I've made a whole row of little rounds, with squares inside them, and I am going to colour the squares yellow, and the bits inside the rounds are going to be blue. It will be a lovely pattern when it's finished. I shall make it all over the page.'

'Yes – it *is* lovely!' said Betty. 'I think I'll do that pattern too!'

'No,' said Harry. 'You mustn't. It's *my* pattern, the one *I* thought of. You mustn't copy it.'

'No, you must think of one for yourself,' said Peggy. 'Look at mine, Betty. Do you like it?'

Betty looked at Peggy's. She had drawn a pattern of ivy leaves all over her page, joining them together with stalks. It was really lovely.

'Oh, dear – I do, *do* wish I could think of a lovely pattern too,' said Betty.

But do you know, by the end of the lesson poor Betty still sat with an empty page before her! She hadn't drawn anything. Miss Brown was cross.

'That is really naughty, Betty,' she said. 'You must

take your pattern book home with you, and think of a pattern to bring me tomorrow morning. You have wasted half an hour.'

Betty was very upset. She badly wanted to cry. She worked very hard in the next lesson, but all the time she was thinking of whether or not she would be able to bring Miss Brown a lovely pattern the next day. She was sure she wouldn't be able to.

'It's snowing!' said Harry suddenly. 'Oh, Miss Brown, look – it's snowing!'

Everyone looked out of the window. Big white snowflakes came floating down without a sound.

'The snow is so quiet,' said Betty. 'That's what I love so much about it.'

'It will be lovely to go home in the snow,' said Harry. 'Miss Brown, isn't it fun to look up into the sky when it is snowing and see millions and millions of snowflakes coming down? Where do they come from?'

'Well,' said Miss Brown, 'when the clouds float through very cold air, they become frozen. Sometimes, you know, the clouds turn into raindrops. But when there is frost about, they turn into tiny ice crystals instead – and these join together and make a big snowflake. It has to fall down, because light though it is, it is too heavy to float in the sky.'

'Snowflakes look like pieces of cloud,' said Harry. 'Bits of frozen mist – how lovely!'

Betty thought it was lovely too. As she went home through the snow, she looked up into the sky. It was full of falling flakes, silent and slow and beautiful.

The little girl lost her way in the snow. She suddenly knew she was lost, and she leant against a tree and began to cry.

'What's the matter?' said a little voice, and Betty saw a small man, dressed just like a magical brownie, all in brown from top to toe.

'Everything's gone wrong today!' said Betty, sobbing. 'I've lost my way in the snow – and Miss Brown was very cross with me because I couldn't think of a pattern.'

'What sort of pattern?' asked the magical brownie in surprise. 'Why do you have to think of patterns?'

Betty told him. 'It's something we do at school. We make up our own patterns, draw them and colour them. It's fun to do it if you are clever at thinking of patterns. But I'm not.'

'But why do you bother to think of them?' asked the magical brownie. 'There are lovely patterns all round you. A daisy flower makes a lovely pattern – so does a pretty oak leaf.'

'There aren't any daisies or oak leaves about now,' said Betty. 'I can't copy those.'

'Well, look – you've got a most wonderful pattern on your sleeve!' said the magical brownie suddenly. 'Look! Look!'

Betty saw a snowflake caught on the sleeve of her black coat. She looked at it hard.

'Have you got good eyes?' said the magical brownie. 'Can you see that the snowflake is made up of tiny crystals – oh, very tiny?'

'Yes, I can,' said Betty, looking hard. 'Oh, what lovely patterns they are, magical brownie! Oh, I do wish I could see them get bigger!'

'I'll get my magic glass for you,' said the magical brownie, and he suddenly opened a door in a tree, went inside, and hopped out again with a round glass that had a handle.

'It's a magnifying glass,' said Betty. 'My granny has one when she wants to read the newspaper. She holds it over the print and it makes all the letters look big, so that she can easily read them.'

'Well, this will make the snow crystals look much bigger to you,' said the magical brownie. He held the glass over Betty's black sleeve – and the little girl cried out in delight.

'Oh! Oh! They are beautiful! Oh, magical brownie, they are the loveliest shapes!'

'But they are all alike in one way although they are all quite different,' said the magical brownie. 'Look at them carefully, and count how many sides each little crystal has got, Betty.'

Betty counted. 'How funny! They all have six sides!' she said. 'All of them. Not one of them has four or five or seven sides – they all have six!'

'Ice crystals always do,' said the magical brownie. 'But although they always have to have six sides, you won't find one ice crystal that is like another. They all grow into a different six-sided pattern. Isn't that marvellous?'

'It's like magic,' said Betty. 'Just like magic. Oh – the snowflake has melted into water! The ice crystals have gone. Quick – I want to see some more. I'll catch another snowflake on my black sleeve.'

Soon she was looking at yet more tiny crystals through the glass. They all had six sides, each one was different and they were beautiful.

'Magical brownie,' said Betty suddenly, 'I shall choose these ice crystals for the pattern I have to do for Miss Brown. Oh, they will make a most wonderful pattern! I can make a different pattern for every page in my drawing book – patterns much lovelier than any of the other children draw. Oh, I do feel excited!'

'I'll show you the way home,' said the magical brownie. 'I'm glad you are pleased about the ice crystals. It's funny you didn't know about them. You'll be able to make fine patterns now!'

Betty went home. She thought of the lovely six-sided crystals she had seen, and she began to draw them very carefully.

She drew a page of this pattern. Then she turned over and drew a page of a second pattern, choosing another ice crystal whose shape she remembered.

Mother came to see. 'Betty, what a lovely pattern!' she said. 'Quite perfect! How *did* you think of it!'

'I didn't,' said Betty. 'I saw it on my black sleeve, out in the snow. It's a six-sided ice crystal, Mother. Oh, Mother, where is Granny's magnifying glass? Do take it out into the snow and look through it at a snowflake on your sleeve! Then you will see how different all the ice crystals are – and yet each one has six sides. There is no end to the shapes and patterns they make.'

Miss Brown was full of surprise when she saw Betty's patterns the next day. 'You didn't do these, dear, surely!' she said. 'Why, even I couldn't think of patterns like this. They are wonderful.'

'I'll show you where to find them,' said Betty happily. 'It's snowing, Miss Brown. Come out with me – and all the others too – and I'll show you where I found these beautiful patterns!'

She took them out into the snow, and they saw what she had seen. You will want to see it too, of course. So remember, next time it snows, go out with a bit of black cloth and catch a snowflake. You'll get such a surprise when you see the beautiful six-sided crystals in the flake.

The Cold
Snowman

The Cold
Snowman

IT HAPPENED ONCE that some children built a great big snowman. You should have seen him! He was as tall as you, but much fatter, and he wore an old top hat, so he looked very grand. On his hands were woollen gloves, but they were rather holey. Down his front were large round pebbles for buttons and round his neck was an old woollen scarf. He really looked very grand indeed.

The children went indoors at teatime, and didn't come out again because it was dark. So the snowman stood all alone in the backyard, and he was very lonely.

He began to sigh, and Foolish-One, the little elf who lived under the old apple tree, heard him and felt sorry. He ran out and spoke to the snowman.

'Are you lonely?' he asked.

'Very,' answered the snowman.

'Are you cold?' asked Foolish-One.

'Who wouldn't be in this frosty weather?' said the snowman.

'I'm sorry for you,' said Foolish-One. 'Shall I sing to you?'

'If you like,' said the snowman. So the elf began to sing a doleful little song about a star that fell from the sky and couldn't get back. It was so sad that the snowman cried a few tears, and they froze at once on his white, snowy cheeks.

'Stop singing that song,' he begged the elf. 'It makes me cry, and it is very painful to do that when your tears freeze on you. Oooh! Isn't the wind cold?'

'Poor snowman!' said Foolish-One, tying the snowman's scarf so tightly that he nearly choked.

'Don't do that!' gasped the snowman. 'You're strangling me.'

'You have no coat,' said Foolish-One, looking sadly at the snowman. 'You will be frozen stiff before morning.'

'Oooh!' said the snowman in alarm. 'Frozen stiff! That sounds dreadful! I wish I wasn't so cold.'

'Shall I get you a nice warm coat?' asked the elf. 'I have one that would keep you very cosy.'

'Well, seeing that you only come up to my knees, I'm afraid that your coat would only be big enough for a handkerchief for me,' said the snowman. 'Oooh! There's that cold wind again.'

Just then a smell of burning came over the air, and the elf sniffed it. He jumped to his feet in excitement. Just the thing!

'Snowman!' he cried. 'There's a bonfire. I can smell it. Let us go to it and warm ourselves.'

The snowman tried to move. He was very heavy, and little bits of snow broke off him. But at last he managed to shuffle along somehow, and he followed the dancing elf down the garden path to the corner of the garden where the bonfire was burning.

'Here we are!' said the elf in delight. 'See what a fine blaze there is. Come, snowman, draw close, and I will tell you a story.'

The snowman came as close to the fire as he could. It was certainly very warm. He couldn't feel the cold wind at all now. It was much better.

'Once upon a time,' began the elf, 'there was a princess called Marigold. Are you nice and warm, snowman?'

'Very,' said the snowman drowsily. The heat was making him sleepy. 'Go on, Foolish-One.'

'Now this princess lived in a high castle,' went on Foolish-One, leaning against the snowman as he talked. 'And one day – are you sure you're quite warm, snowman?'

'Very, very warm,' murmured the snowman, his hat slipping to one side of his head. Plonk! One of his stone buttons fell off. Plonk! Then another. How odd!

Foolish-One went on with his story. It wasn't a very exciting one, and the snowman hardly listened. He was so warm and sleepy. Foolish-One suddenly felt sleepy too. He stopped in the middle of his tale and shut his eyes. Then very gently he began to snore.

He woke up with a dreadful jump, for he heard a most peculiar noise.

Sizzle-sizzle-sizzle, *ss-ss-sss-ss*!

Whatever could it be? He jumped up. The fire was almost out. The snowman had gone! Only his hat, scarf and gloves remained, and they were in a pile on the ground.

'Who has put the fire out?' cried Foolish-One in a rage. 'Snowman, where are you? Why have you gone off and left all your clothes? You will catch your death of cold!'

But the snowman didn't answer. He was certainly quite gone. Foolish-One began to cry. The fire was quite out now, and a pool of water lay all round it. Who had poured the water there? And where, oh where, was that nice snowman?

He called him up the garden and down. He hunted for him everywhere. Then he went home and found his thickest coat and warmest hat. He put them on, took his stick and went out.

'I will find that snowman if it takes me a thousand years to do it!' he cried. And off he went to begin his search. He hasn't found him yet! Poor Foolish-One, I don't somehow think he ever will!

The Lucky
Number

The Lucky Number

THE TWINS SAT at the nursery window and talked about Christmas presents.

'We know what to give Daddy,' said Paul. 'He wants some chocolate.'

'And Nurse wants a pincushion; I asked her today,' said Pamela. 'And Jane would love a new frilly cap, Mummy said so.'

'We've got a bunny for baby, and a picture for Auntie Madge, and a lovely red tie for Uncle Dick,' went on Paul. 'There's only Mummy left. What *can* we give her?'

'She says she wants two kettle-holders,' answered Pamela, 'but I know she only says that because she thinks we haven't got much money left. But we have, we've got lots – three shillings and fourpence ha'penny.'

'Let's go and ask her again,' said Paul. So the twins ran downstairs, and were just going into the drawing room when they heard Mummy talking to a visitor.

'Don't go in yet,' said Pamela, 'perhaps she's just going away.'

So they stood and waited outside the door, whispering to each other. But suddenly they heard Mummy say something which made them both listen hard.

'That *is* a dear little gold watch you've got, Mrs Jones,' said Mummy. 'I wish I had one like it. But there always seem so many things to buy for the house and for the children that I've never agreed to let my husband give me one. It seems such a lot of money to spend on myself!'

'I got this one at those big new Stores in the town,' said Mrs Jones. 'It's a real beauty. They have a fine jewellery department there.'

'Quick! Come back upstairs!' whispered Paul,

pulling Pamela away. 'We know what Mummy wants now – a gold watch!'

'Yes, but will three shillings and fourpence ha'penny buy one?' asked Pamela doubtfully.

'I expect so,' answered Paul. 'Anyway, perhaps they'd let us have one cheap!'

Just then there was a big bang at the front door.

'The postman!' screamed the twins excitedly.

But it wasn't. It was Uncle Dick, big and jolly, and he caught hold of both of the twins and put them one on each shoulder.

'Now then, you rascals!' he cried. 'Go and get your coats on and come out Christmas shopping with me. Santa Claus is at the big Stores in the town this afternoon, and I expect you'd like to see him! He's going to give somebody a big surprise.'

The twins shrieked with joy, and ran off to get their things. Then away down the street they went with Uncle Dick, hopping and skipping and both talking at once.

When they got to the Stores, Santa Claus was standing at the door.

'Good afternoon, little people,' he said, and bowed very low. 'Would you like to put your name against one of these numbers in my little book?'

'What for?' asked Paul shyly.

'Well, we're going to put a lot of numbers in a hat, and then I'm going to pick some out,' said Santa Claus. 'The first number I draw out may perhaps be 63. I look in my book to see who has put their name against number 63. Perhaps it might be you. If it is, then you can come round the shop with me, and choose anything you like for a present up to the value of ten pounds!'

'We'll *all* put our names in your book,' said Uncle Dick, giving Santa Claus some money. 'I'll put my name against number 42. That's the number of my house!'

'And I'll have 84, because that's the number of *my* house,' cried Pamela.

'What shall *I* have, then?' Paul asked.

'Have number 7, that's just how old you are,' said Pamela.

'I'm afraid someone else has put his name against that number,' Santa Claus told them.

'I'll have 29, then,' said Paul, writing his name. 'That's how old my mummy is!'

'Now I want to go to the place where they sell jewellery,' said Paul. So off they went.

'Show me some gold watches, please,' said Paul, when they got there.

'Here, old son!' exclaimed Uncle Dick. 'You haven't got enough money for gold watches!'

But the shop girl had brought a big trayful, and put it down in front of the twins.

'Oh-h! This is the one Mummy would like!' cried Pamela, picking up a tiny square-faced watch, with a gold bracelet attached to it.

'How much is it?' asked Paul.

'Eight pounds!' answered the shop girl.

'Oh, dear! And we've only got three shillings and fourpence ha'penny!' sighed Paul. 'Could you let us have it cheap, do you think? We'll give you the money straight away – now, if you like.'

The girl shook her head and smiled, and Uncle Dick told her to take the watches away.

'You must think of something else for Mummy!' he said. 'A watch is much too dear. Let's go and have some tea.'

They had a glorious tea, and afterwards went into the toy part of the shop and had a splendid time looking at everything. Uncle Dick bought some mysterious presents, which he wouldn't let them see, though they begged him to show them.

'Wait till Christmas!' he chuckled. 'Now come along home. Oh, wait a minute – there's Santa Claus picking out numbers from a hat. Let's just stay and see if any of us have been lucky!'

The twins watched Santa Claus put his hand into a hat in which were little bits of paper, each with a number on. He stirred them round and round and looked at the people with a smile.

'Which number will it be?' he said, and drew out a slip of paper.

'It's number 29!' he called, and looked in his book. 'Paul Paterson chose that number. Where is lucky Paul Paterson?'

'Here! Here!' shouted Paul, waving his hand and jumping up and down wildly.

'Well, Paul Paterson, wait a minute till I see who wins the second and third prizes!' said Santa Claus, smiling. 'Then you shall come round the shop with me and choose what you want. You'd better be deciding.'

Of course, you can guess what Paul chose! He went to the jewellery department with jolly old Santa Claus, and he chose that dear little square-faced watch for Mummy!

'Wouldn't you rather have that beautiful model aeroplane, or that glorious little birch-bark canoe?' asked Santa Claus in astonishment.

'No, thank you. I know Mummy wants a gold watch, and now I've got it for her. Oh, Pamela, isn't it lovely! We'll give it to her together, of course! Come on, Uncle Dick! Oh, you *are* a darling to have taken us out this afternoon!' And Paul gave his uncle the tightest hug he could manage.

And you can just guess what a simply glorious surprise Mummy got on Christmas morning. A gold watch! She could hardly believe her eyes!

The Little Fir Tree

The Little Fir Tree

ONCE UPON A time there was a little fir tree not much bigger than you. It grew in a forest on the mountainside. It was an evergreen, so it did not drop all its narrow green leaves in the autumn, but held on to some of them all the year round.

Many little fir trees grew around it. Nearby were some full-grown firs, tall and straight and strong. Sometimes men came to cut them down and to send them away. Then the little fir tree would wonder where they were going, and would feel sad.

'It is dreadful to be cut down,' said the little tree.

'Dreadful to have our branches sawn off, and to be nothing but a straight pole!'

'Do not be sad,' said a big fir tree nearby. 'We are going to be made into straight telegraph poles – and some of us will be the masts of ships. Ah, that's a grand end for a fir tree – to be planted in a ship, and to hold the flapping sails that send the ship along!'

The little fir tree thought that would indeed be a grand life. It hoped that when it had grown tall and straight it too would end as a mast in a ship.

It would be grand to drive along over the water, hearing the wind once again, being of use for many, many years, thought the little fir tree.

All the small growing fir trees hoped the same thing, and they grew a little each year. Then one winter there came a great storm.

It broke on the mountainside where the forest of fir trees grew. It sent a great wind blowing through their branches.

'We shall fall, we shall fall!' said the fir trees, and their branches tossed and shouted in the wind.

'We have no deep roots!' they said. 'Do not blow so hard, wind! You will blow us over!'

'You should grow big deep roots,' said the wind. 'I cannot uproot the strong oak, because it sends its roots deep down. But your roots are too near the surface!'

One big fir tree gave a deep groan. The wind had blown so strongly against it that it was pulled right out of the ground. It toppled over – it fell!

It crashed against the next fir tree and made that fall too. That one fell against a third tree, and down this went as well. Crash! Crash! Crash!

Each falling tree hit the one next to it, and soon many were falling, like a row of dominoes, through the forest. The last one fell on the little fir tree, and pulled it up by its roots.

The gale died down. The sun came out. Men came into the forest to see what trees had been blown down.

'Look – a great path has been made in the forest, by one tree uprooting the next,' said one of the men. 'We will clear away the fallen trees.'

So, very soon, the sound of axes was heard in the forest, and one after another of the fallen trees was chopped away from its roots, its branches trimmed off, and it was taken away to be made into a telegraph pole or the mast of a ship.

The men came to the little fir tree, which had been uprooted by the last falling tree. 'Look,' said one, 'here is a young tree uprooted. It is almost dead.'

'Give it a chance,' said another man. 'We will replant it and see if it will grow.'

So they put the little fir tree back into the ground and stamped down the earth around its roots.

The little tree was almost dead. Its roots were half frozen. It felt ill and weak.

But soon its roots took firm hold of the earth again, and began to feed the tree. It felt better. Its branches stiffened a little. It put its topmost spike straight. All spruce firs have a spear at the top, which they stick straight upwards to the sky. The little fir tree was glad to point its spike up again too.

But, because it had been uprooted for so long, the little fir tree did not grow well. It was short and stunted. It did not grow freely upwards as the other young trees did. It remained small and short, not much bigger than you.

'You must try to grow,' said the other trees. 'If you don't, you will be pulled up and burnt, for you will be of no use to anyone. Try to grow, little fir tree.'

'I am trying,' said the little tree. 'But something has happened to me. I am afraid I shall always be small. I have lost the power of growing.'

It did grow a very little – but by the time the other firs were tall and straight, the little fir tree was very tiny still. It was sad.

'I know I shall be thrown away,' it said to itself. 'I know I shall. I did want to be of some use in the world – but now I shan't be. When the men come to look at

the other young trees they will think they are fine –
but they are sure to pull me up.'

Sure enough, when the men came round just
before Christmas, they were very pleased with the
other young firs – but they did not think much of
the little one.

'This is a poor tree,' said one. 'It will never be
any good.'

They went on into the forest. But later on one of the
men came back to the little fir tree. He dug round its
roots, and then pulled it out of the ground. He put it
over his shoulder.

'Goodbye!' called the little fir tree to all its friends.
'Goodbye! I am going to be thrown away. I am of no
use. But I wanted to be; I did want to be!'

The man walked down the mountainside with the
little tree. He came to a cosy house, with lights shining
from the windows, for it was almost dark. He stamped
into the house, shook the snow off his shoulders and
called loudly, 'Peter! Ann! I've got something for you!'

Two children came running out, and they shouted for joy to see the little fir tree. 'Oh, what a dear little tree! It's just the right size!'

Then a good many things happened that puzzled the little fir tree very much. It was put into a big tub. The tub was wound round and round with bright red silk, and looked very merry.

Then clips were put on the branches of the little tree, and candles were stuck into the clips! Soon it had candles from top to bottom!

Then bright, shining ornaments were hung from every branch. Some were blue, some were red, some were green and some were yellow. They were very lovely, made of the finest glass.

'I am beautiful!' said the little tree in surprise. 'I may be small and undergrown – but how lovely I am, dressed in these shining things! How the children must love me!'

Then other things were hung on the little tree – presents wrapped in bright paper. Some of them pulled down the branches, for they were heavy, but the little tree didn't mind. It was too happy to mind anything.

Strings of glittering tinsel were hung everywhere on the tree. And then, at the very top, a wonderful fairy doll was put, with a silver crown and wand, and a fluffy frock that stood out all round her.

'I never saw such a beautiful tree as you!' said the fairy doll. 'Never! I am proud to be at the top of you. You have a nice straight spike there that I can lean against.'

'All spruce firs have those spikes at the top,' said the fir tree proudly. 'That is how you can tell us from other fir trees. Why have the children made me so beautiful, little doll?'

'You are their Christmas tree!' said the doll. 'Didn't you know that children take little fir trees at Christmas time, dress them up and hang their presents there? Ah, it is a wonderful thing to be a Christmas tree, and bring happiness and joy to many people.'

'I am glad I didn't grow,' said the little tree. 'Oh, I

am glad I didn't grow. Once I wanted to be the mast of a ship. Now I am glad to be a Christmas tree.'

It shone softly when the candles were lit. 'We have never had such a lovely Christmas tree before,' said Peter. 'Isn't it beautiful? Its branches are just the right size. It is a dear little tree.'

'We will plant it out in the garden when Christmas is over,' said their mother. 'Then it will take root there – and maybe next year we can dig it up again and have it once more for our tree!'

'And the year after – and the year after!' cried the children.

So I expect they will. What a lovely life for the little fir tree – to grow in the wind and the sun all the year, and to be a shining Christmas tree in the winter!

Bobbo's Magic
Stocking

Bobbo's Magic Stocking

ONCE UPON A time, many years ago, there was a little boy called Bobbo. He lived with his father and mother in a nice house in London, and he had plenty of toys and plenty of pets.

In the house he had his puppy, Jock, and his kitten, Snowball, and two yellow canaries. In the garden he had two pet rabbits, and a chicken that laid him a brown egg every morning as regular as clockwork.

In the nursery was a tall rocking horse and a bookcase with twenty books of adventure and fairy tales in it. In the toy cupboard were balls, railway trains, bricks, teddy bears, clowns, a box of paints and a cricket bat. So you wouldn't think that Bobbo wanted anything else at all, would you?

But he did! He was always wanting something new. He was always tired of what he had got.

'Mummy, buy me this,' he would say, or, 'Daddy, buy me that!'

'You've got quite enough things,' said his parents, but more often than not they were foolish enough to buy Bobbo what he wanted, so that his toy cupboard was full almost to bursting.

The worst of it was that Bobbo would never give any of his toys away unless he was made to. He was a selfish little boy, who couldn't really be bothered to think about anybody else.

'I don't know how to cure him,' said his mother with a sigh.

'And I don't know how to cure him,' said his father with a frown.

But he *was* cured, and you will soon see how.

It happened that one night, about a week before

Christmas Day, Bobbo was in bed, and couldn't get to sleep. He tried and he tried, but it was no use. He heard the clock in the hall strike nine, and ten, and then he heard his father and mother come up to bed. After a long time the clock struck eleven, and Bobbo knew that in an hour's time it would be midnight.

Fairies and elves come out at midnight, he thought to himself. 'I've never been awake at twelve o'clock before, so perhaps I may see or hear something surprising. I'll listen.'

He lay in bed and listened to the sounds of the night. He heard the wind come whistling in at his window, and an owl hoot loudly. Then he heard another sound, a curious one that made him sit up, feeling puzzled.

It was the sound of sleigh bells, jingling in the distance! Nearer they came and nearer, and Bobbo jumped out of bed and ran to the window. It was a bright moonlit night, and he could see quite well down the snowy street. First of all, in the distance, he saw something coming along that looked like a carriage drawn by horses. And then he saw what it really was!

It was Santa Claus's sleigh, drawn by four fine reindeer with great branching antlers! The bells on the reins jingled loudly, but the reindeer themselves made no noise as they trotted along in the deep snow. Driving them was a large elf, and at the back, in the big sleigh, was a crowd of laughing children, all in their nightclothes, the boys in pyjamas and the girls in their frilly nightdresses.

Bobbo stared in astonishment. The sleigh came nearer and nearer, and then, just outside Bobbo's gate, it stopped. The elf threw the reins on to the backs of the reindeer, and then took up a big book and opened it. He ran his finger down a page, and then nodded his head as if he had found what he wanted.

He stepped down from the sleigh, and ran through the gate of the house next to Bobbo's.

Oh, he's gone to fetch Nancy from next door, thought Bobbo. *I suppose he's fetching all the children who have been extra good, to take them for a trip to Fairyland, or somewhere. Well, I'm sure he won't fetch me, because I know I haven't been good for quite a week. Still, I don't see why I shouldn't go and have a look at that sleigh. I'm quite certain it's the one that Santa Claus uses and I don't expect I'll ever get another chance of seeing it so close.*

He put on his slippers, and ran down the stairs. He slipped the bolts of the front door, and then opened it. Out he went into the moonlight, feeling not in the least cold, for it was fairy weather that night.

Bobbo saw that the elf had not yet come back from the house next door, so he ran down the path to his front gate. He saw that the sleigh was a very big one, and that the reindeer were the loveliest he had ever seen.

As he ran up, the children in the sleigh leant out and saw him. They waved happily to him, and called him.

'Come along,' they said. 'Have you been a good boy too?'

Bobbo stopped and looked at the children in the

sleigh. He saw that they thought he was one of the good children that the elf was fetching. Quick as a flash Bobbo made up his mind to let them go on thinking so, for he thought that perhaps he would be able to go with them on the trip, if the elf did not see that he was an extra child.

He nodded and laughed to the children, and they put out their hands to him, and pulled him into the sleigh with them.

'Isn't it fun?' they said. 'Isn't it fun?'

'Where are we going?' asked Bobbo.

'Oh, don't you know?' said a golden-haired boy. 'We're going to visit the place where Santa Claus lives, and see all the toys being made! He always sends his elf to fetch good children every year, and this year it's *our* turn!'

'Here comes the elf!' cried a little girl. 'He's got a dear little smiling girl with him! Make room for her!' All the children squashed up to make room for Nancy. Bobbo got right at the back of the sleigh, for he didn't want the elf to see him, and he felt sure that if Nancy spied him, she might make some remark about him. Nancy sat down in the front, and began to talk to all the children in an excited little voice.

'Now we're off again!' cried the elf, climbing into the driving seat. 'Hold tight!'

He jerked the reins, and the reindeer started off again over the snow, pulling the sleigh so smoothly that Bobbo felt as if he was in a dream. Now that he really was off with the children he felt a little bit uncomfortable, for he didn't know what the elf might say when he found that he had one boy too many.

The sleigh went on and on and on, through the town and into the country. At last it stopped again before a tiny little cottage, and once more the elf looked in his address book, and found the names he wanted.

'There are two children to come from here,' he said, 'and then that's all. After we've got them, we'll go straight off to the home of Santa Claus, and see all the wonderful things he has to show you!'

He went through the gate and tapped softly at the door of the cottage. It was opened at once, and Bobbo saw two excited children standing there, one a girl and one a boy.

'Come on, twins,' said the elf cheerfully. 'The sleigh is waiting.'

The two children ran to the sleigh, and jumped in. The elf once more took up the reins, and the sleigh began to move very quickly over the snow.

'Hold on as tightly as you can!' said the elf. 'I'm going to go at top speed, for we're a little late!'

All the children held on to each other and gasped in delight as the sleigh tore along over the snow at a most tremendous rate. The wind whistled by, and blew their hair straight out behind them, so that they laughed to see each other.

'Look at that hill!' the golden-haired boy cried suddenly. 'It's like a cliff, it's so steep!'

Bobbo looked, and he saw a most enormous hill stretching up in front of the sleigh. It was very, very steep, but the reindeer leapt up it as easily as if it was level ground. The sleigh tilted backwards, and the children held on more tightly than ever. Up and up went the sleigh, right to the very, very top, and then, on the summit, drenched in moonlight, it stopped.

'We've come to a little inn!' cried one of the children, leaning out. 'Oh, and here come six little gnomes, carrying something! What *are* they going to do?'

All the children leant out to watch. They saw the gnomes come hurrying up, carrying pairs of lovely green wings. There were six pairs of these, and the gnomes knew just what to do with them.

Four of the gnomes went to the reindeer, and fastened a pair of wings on to their backs. The other two bent down by the sleigh, and the children saw that they had fastened two pairs of wings on to the sides of the sleigh as well!

'We're going to fly, we're going to fly!' they cried. 'Oh, what fun it will be!'

When the wings were all tightly fastened the gnomes

stepped back. The elf driver gathered up the reins once more, and the reindeer plunged forward.

Bobbo looked all round. He could see a long, long way from the top of the steep hill, and the world looked very lovely in the silver moonlight. As the sleigh started forward again he saw that, instead of going down the other side of the hill, they had jumped straight off it, and were now galloping steadily through the air!

My word! thought Bobbo. *Now we're off to Santa Claus's home! I do wonder what it will be like.*

The sleigh went on and on for a very long time, but the children didn't get at all tired, for they loved looking downwards and seeing the towns, villages, lakes and seas they passed over. The elf answered their questions, and told them all they wanted to know.

'Do you see that great mountain sticking up into the sky?' he said at last. 'Well, that is where Santa Claus lives. In five minutes we shall be there.'

Bobbo began to wonder if he would be found out by Santa Claus when he arrived.

Perhaps he won't notice, he thought. *There are so many children in the sleigh that surely he won't see there is one too many!*

Nearer and nearer to the mountain glided the sleigh, and at last it touched the summit. The reindeer felt their feet on firm ground once more, and the children shouted in delight.

On top of the mountain was built an enormous castle, its towers shining against the moonlit sky. Just as the sleigh bumped gently down to the ground, a big jolly man came running out of the great open door of the castle. He was dressed in red, and had big boots on and a pointed red hat.

'Santa Claus! Santa Claus!' cried all the children, and they scrambled out of the sleigh, and rushed to meet him as fast as they could. Bobbo quite forgot that he wasn't supposed to be there, and ran to meet him too.

The jolly old man swung the children off their feet and hugged them.

'Pleased to see you,' he said. 'What a fine batch of good children this year!'

Then Bobbo remembered. He slipped behind the twins, and said nothing. He was terribly afraid of being found out and sent home before he had seen all he wanted to.

'Come along!' cried Santa Claus. 'There's some hot cocoa and chocolate buns waiting for you. Then we'll all go and visit my toy workshops.'

He led the way into the castle. The children followed him into a great big hall, with a log fire burning at one end. Before the fire was a big fur rug, and the children all sat down on it, and waited for their buns and cocoa. Magical brownies ran in with trays full of cups, and soon all the children were drinking and eating, talking and laughing in the greatest excitement.

'Now, have you finished?' asked Santa Claus. 'Well,

come along then, all of you. We'll go to the rocking-horse workshop first.'

Off they all trooped. Santa Claus led them down a long passage towards the sound of hammering and clattering. He opened a big door, and there was the rocking-horse workshop!

It was the loveliest place! There were gnomes running about with hammers and paint pots, and everyone was working at top speed.

'Only a week before Christmas,' explained Santa Claus. 'We're very busy just now. I've had so many letters from children asking for rocking horses this year that I had to have a good many hundreds more made than usual. Go round and see my gnomes at work.'

The children wandered round, watching the busy gnomes. Bobbo went with the golden-haired boy, and they saw the horses being carefully painted. One gnome was very busy sticking fine bushy tails on to the horses, and another one was putting on the manes.

Two little gnomes were doing the nicest work of all. They were going round the workshop, riding first on one horse, then on another, to see if they all rocked properly.

'How do you get the horses on to the sleigh?' asked Bobbo.

'Watch!' said the gnome he spoke to. He climbed up on to a rocking horse and jerked the reins quickly. At once the horse seemed to come alive, and rocked swiftly forward over the floor before Bobbo could say 'Knife!' It went towards the door all by itself, neighing loudly, while the little gnome waved his hand to Bobbo. All the other horses began to neigh when they heard the first one, and the children stared in astonishment as they saw first one and then another come alive and begin to sway forward. Only those that were not quite finished kept still.

'Catch a rocking horse and get on to its back!' cried Santa Claus. 'We'll let them take us to my next workshop – where the doll's houses are made!'

Every child caught hold of a rocking horse and climbed on to its back. Bobbo got a fine one, painted in red and green with a great bushy tail and mane. He took hold of the reins, and at once the horse rocked quickly forwards, following Santa Claus, who had jumped on to the biggest horse there. Off they all went on their strange horses, and rocked all the way upstairs to another big room.

'Here we are,' said Santa Claus. 'Now see how carefully your doll's houses are made, children!'

The children jumped off their horses and stared in wonder. The room was full of little fairies, who were doing all sorts of jobs. Some were daintily painting the roof of a doll's house, and others were cleaning the windows.

There must be thousands and thousands of houses, thought Bobbo, looking round. *Oh, there's a fairy putting up curtains! I often wondered who put those tiny curtains up at the windows of doll's houses!* He went round looking at everything. He saw curtains being put up, knockers being polished, pictures hung and carpets laid.

'The fairies do all this because they're just the right size to get into the houses nicely,' said Santa Claus. 'Look! Here are some houses being lived in to see if they are quite free from damp, and have been well built.'

The children looked. They had come to one end of the big room, where a whole row of doll's houses stood side by side. As they looked they saw the front doors open, and out came a number of little fairies.

'We sleep in the beds and see if they are comfortable,' they told the children. 'We cook our dinners on the stove in the kitchen and see if it is all right. We sit on all the chairs to see if they are soft. Then, if they are, we know your dolls will enjoy themselves here. And even if you don't let your dolls live in these houses, well, the fairies who live in your nurseries will often spend a night or two there, and they will be glad to find everything all right.'

Bobbo would have liked to stay there all night,

watching the fairies pop in and out of the doll's houses, but Santa Claus told the children to mount their rocking horses again, and follow him.

'We'll go to the train workshop now!' he said. And off they all galloped again on their trusty wooden horses, downstairs and round a corner into a great yard.

'My goodness!' said Bobbo, when he got there. 'What a lot of trains!'

There *were* a lot too! They were all rushing round and round, or up and down, driven by pixies.

'We've finished making all these,' said Santa Claus. 'They're ready to go to children now, but the pixies are just testing them to see that they run all right.'

Bobbo thought it was grand to test toy trains like that. The pixies seemed to be enjoying themselves immensely. They were very clever at driving their little trains, and never bumped into each other. They went under little bridges and past little signals at a terrific rate, their engines dragging behind them a long procession of carriages or trucks.

'Oh, they stop at the little stations!' cried the golden-haired boy. 'Look!'

Sure enough they did! There were tiny stations here and there with metal porters standing by trucks, and metal passengers waiting. And they all came alive when the engine stopped at their station! The porters began wheeling their trucks, and the passengers ran to get in the carriages.

'Oh, isn't it fun!' cried the children. 'How we wish we could ride in a little toy train too!'

'Very well, you can!' laughed Santa Claus. 'The metal ones are too small, but I've a big wooden train and carriages here that will just about take you all. Here it comes.'

The children saw a big red wooden engine coming along, driven by a pixie. It dragged three open wooden carriages behind it, and stopped by Santa Claus.

'Get in!' he said. 'There's room for all of you. We'll go to the next workshop in the train and tell the horses to go back to their own place.'

At once the rocking horses rocked themselves away, and the children climbed into the carriages of the wooden train. It was just large enough for them, and when they were all in, it trundled away merrily.

It took them to where the clockwork toys were made, and after that to where the red gnomes were making fireworks. Then they went to where the dolls were made, and the teddy bears and soft toys. And soon they had visited so many exciting places that Bobbo began to lose count, and became more excited than ever.

But at last they came to the only place they hadn't seen. This was a big room, in the middle of which a beautiful fairy was sitting. She sat by a well that went deep down into the mountain, so deep that no one knew how deep it was. No one had ever heard a stone reach the bottom.

'Now this,' said Santa Claus, 'is the Wishing Well.' All the children looked at it in awe.

None of them had seen a wishing well before, and the fairy by it was so beautiful that she almost dazzled their eyes.

'All the good children who come here year by year,' said Santa Claus, 'visit this Well before they go back home. The fairy who owns it gives them one wish. She will give you each one, so think hard before you wish, for whatever your wish is it will come true.'

The children stared at each other, and thought of what they would wish. Then one by one they stepped forwards. The fairy handed them each a little blue stone, and told them to drop it into the Well as they spoke their wish.

The golden-haired boy wished first.

'I wish that my mother may get well before Christmas,' he said.

Then came the twins and they wished together.

'We wish our father could get some work to do,' they wished.

Then came other children, all wishing differently.

'I wish my mummy had lots of nice things for Christmas,' said one.

'I wish my little brother may not be ill any more,' said another.

'I wish all the poor children in my town a big Christmas pudding on Christmas Day,' said a third.

So the wishes went on, until it came to Bobbo's turn. He had been thinking very hard what he would wish for, and being a selfish little boy, he thought of nobody but himself.

He went up to the fairy, and took the blue stone she held out to him. Then he turned to the Well, and dropped it in.

'I wish that on Christmas Day I may have a Christmas stocking that will pour out toys and pets for me without stopping!' he said.

At once there was a dead silence. Everybody stared at Bobbo, and he began to feel uncomfortable.

Then the fairy spoke sadly.

'Alas!' she said. 'I have given a wish to a child who is not good, for he is selfish. He will regret his wish on Christmas Day.'

'No, I shan't,' said Bobbo, feeling very glad to think that his wish wasn't going to be taken from him.

'Come here,' said Santa Claus sternly to Bobbo. The little boy went over to him, and Santa Claus looked at him closely.

'You are not one of this year's good children,' he said. 'How did you get here?'

Bobbo hung his head and told him. Santa Claus frowned heavily, and all the watching children trembled.

'You have done a foolish thing,' said Santa Claus, 'and your own foolishness will punish you.' Then he turned to the other children.

'It is time to return home,' he told them. 'We are late, so we will not go by the reindeer sleigh this time. The fairy will wish a wish for you.'

'Come near to me,' said the fairy in her silvery voice. 'Take hands, all of you, and sit down on the ground. Shut your eyes and listen to me.'

They all did as they were told, Bobbo too, and shut their eyes to listen. The fairy began to sing them a dreamy, sleepy song, and soon every child's head fell forward, and one by one the children slept.

Bobbo's head dropped forward on to his chest as he heard the fairy's dreamy voice, and soon he was dreaming. He went on dreaming and dreaming and dreaming, and while he was dreaming, the fairy, by her magic, took him, and all the other children, back to their faraway beds. But how she did it neither I nor anyone knows.

When Bobbo woke up the next morning he rubbed his eyes, and suddenly remembered his adventures of the night before.

I don't think it could *have been a dream*, he thought. *What about my slippers? I had those on, and if they are dirty underneath then I shall know I really* did *go out in the snow with them on!*

He jumped out of bed and went to find his slippers. They were standing by the bed, and when he picked them up, he saw that underneath they were not only dirty, but wet too.

'That just proves it!' said Bobbo in delight. 'Now I shall only have to wait a few days more for my wish to come true. Fancy having a stocking that will pour me out pets and toys without stopping!'

He told nobody about his adventure, and waited impatiently for Christmas Day to come. He wondered where he would find the stocking, and he decided that it would probably be hanging at the end of the bed, where Christmas stockings usually hang.

At last Christmas Eve came. Bobbo went to bed early so that Christmas Day would come all the sooner. He lay for a long time without going to sleep, for he was feeling very excited.

Then at last his eyes closed and he fell asleep. The night flowed by, and dawn came.

Bobbo woke up about seven o'clock and found a grey light in his bedroom. Day had hardly yet come. He remembered at once what was to happen, and he sat up quickly, his heart thumping in excitement. He gazed at the end of his bed, and saw there the Christmas stocking that his father and mother had given him, full of toys. Down on the floor beside it were lots of parcels, but Bobbo didn't feel a bit interested in them. He wanted to see where the magic stocking was.

Then he saw it. It was a little blue stocking, just the colour of the stone he had thrown down the Wishing Well. It hung on one of the knobs of his bed, and looked as thin and empty as his own stocking did, lying on the chair nearby.

'Oh!' cried Bobbo in disappointment. 'Is that all my magic stocking is going to be?'

He reached over to the foot of the bed, and took the stocking down. Then he had a good look at it. It was tied up at the top with a piece of blue ribbon, and the stocking itself felt as empty as could be.

'There's nothing in it at all!' said Bobbo angrily. 'That fairy told a story!'

He took hold of the ribbon that tied up the top of the stocking, and jerked it undone. It came off the stocking and fell on to the bed. Bobbo turned the stocking upside down, and shook it out on to the pillow, thinking there might perhaps be some little thing inside it.

And then the magic began to work! For out of the stocking suddenly came a kitten that fell on the pillow and began to mew! Then came a box of soldiers, and then a book. Bobbo had no time to look at each thing carefully, for before he had time to pick it up, something else came!

'It's working, it's working!' cried the little boy in the greatest excitement. 'Oh my goodness, oh my gracious, it's really, really magic!'

Out came a whole host of things on to his bed! They certainly came from the stocking, though Bobbo could never feel them in there before they appeared. All sorts of things came, big and little, and even a rocking horse suddenly fell with a thump on to the floor!

Soon Bobbo's bed was covered with toys. The kitten mewed as a ball came tumbling on to its head, and no sooner had it mewed than another kitten came falling down by it, and then a puppy and a little yellow canary.

After the canary came a whole string of white rats, about twenty of them. They ran about all over the place, and squeaked loudly. Bobbo watched them in amazement.

But then something happened that made the little boy begin to feel uncomfortable. The stocking suddenly jerked out of his hand, and began to flap about in a most curious manner, all by itself. Out of it came a long leg, with a hoof at the end. Then another appeared and yet another. The stocking jumped nearly up to the ceiling, and when it came down again, Bobbo saw that a great animal was miraculously falling on to the floor too. And whatever in the world do you think it was?

It was a great white donkey, with long black ears. As soon as it reached the floor, it began to make a most alarming sound.

'Hee-haw, hee-haw!' it went, and stamped on the carpet with its hind feet.

'Oh, dear!' cried Bobbo, slipping under the blankets quickly. 'I don't like this. It's too much magic, I think!'

Now Bobbo's father and mother were lying in bed talking, when they suddenly heard the enormous noise made by the donkey in Bobbo's bedroom. Bobbo's father leapt out of bed at once, and his mother sat up in terror.

'Whatever is it?' she cried. 'It sounds as if it's coming from Bobbo's bedroom.'

'I'll go and see,' said his father, and tore down the landing. He flung open the door of Bobbo's room – and then stared in the greatest horror and amazement.

And well he might, for Bobbo's room was full of hundreds and hundreds of things. Toys, big and little, were strewn all over the place, and kittens and puppies were playing madly together. White rats nibbled at the sweets and chocolates down by the bed, and a rabbit was lying on the hearth rug. Worst of all, the donkey stood with its forefeet on the mantelpiece, trying to nibble some carrots in a picture.

Bobbo was nowhere to be seen. He was safely under the blankets, cowering at the bottom of the bed. The stocking lay on the floor, and things jerked themselves out without stopping. Even as Bobbo's horrified father looked, he saw a tortoise come wriggling out, and make its way to where he stood on the mat.

'Oh! Oh!' cried Bobbo's father. 'What is happening here? Bobbo, Bobbo, where are you? Where have you gone?'

Bobbo answered from the bottom of the bed.

'I'm here,' he said. 'Oh, Daddy, is it you? Come and rescue me from all these things.'

His father stepped over six white rats, stumbled over the rabbit, went round the rocking horse, trod on a box of fine soldiers and reached Bobbo. He picked up the little boy, blanket and all, and lifted him up in his arms. Then, nearly falling over a pile of big teddy bears, and squashing two boxes of chocolates, he managed to make his way safely to the door. He carried Bobbo into his mother's room, and told his astonished wife what he had seen.

Even as he spoke, two white rats ran into the room,

and Bobbo's mother shrieked in horror. Then the donkey was heard downstairs, and two screams from below told the parents that the cook, and the housemaid, had seen him.

'What does it all mean, what does it all mean?' cried Bobbo's mother. 'Are we dreaming, or is this all real?'

'Bobbo, do you know anything about this?' asked his father. 'How did it all begin?'

Bobbo began to cry, and in between his tears he told the story of how he had been to the home of Santa Claus, pretending to be one of the good children. He told about his wish, and how it had come true that very morning.

'It's all that horrid magic stocking,' wept Bobbo. 'It's lying in my room bringing out things without stopping, just as I wished it to. Oh, why didn't I wish an unselfish wish like all the other children did?'

Bobbo's mother and father listened to the story gravely. They were grieved to think their little boy had not been good enough to be chosen, but had gone all the same, and had wished a wish that showed what an unpleasant child he was.

'It's our fault really,' said his father to his mother. 'We have spoilt him, you and I. We have always let him think of himself and never of other people. We must alter all that now.'

'I want to alter it,' said Bobbo. 'I want to be good, but I shan't have a chance now. That horrid stocking will go on and on all my life long!'

'Oh, bless us all, I'd forgotten that stocking would still be going on,' said his father, jumping up. 'Hallo, what's that?'

He heard a loud voice shouting up the stairs. It was a policeman!

'Hi, there!' called the deep voice. 'What are you doing, letting your pets out of the house like this? You're frightening all the neighbours! This is a fine sort of Christmas morning to give them. Why, the road's full of puppies, rats and kittens, to say nothing of rabbits, goats and a snake or two.'

Bobbo's father waded through pets and toys until he got downstairs. There he saw the indignant policeman, and found that the cook and the housemaid had run out of the house in fright, and had left the front door open, so that all the pets had been able to wander downstairs and outside.

'Are you thinking of starting a zoo?' asked the puzzled policeman, trying to catch a white rat that was running up his trouser leg.

'No,' said Bobbo's father, 'it's magic, I'm afraid.'

'Come on now!' said the policeman. 'You can't spin a story like that to me!'

A large swan came flying down the stairs and landed on his shoulder. He was so astonished that he fell straight down the front steps with the swan on top of him, and just as he was getting up, something got between his legs, and he sat down on a hedgehog.

That was enough for the policeman. Swans, snakes, hedgehogs and rats seemed to belong to nightmares, not to Christmas morning, so he got off the hedgehog, and ran for his life to the nearest police station.

'Oh, my!' said Bobbo's father, seeing two large tortoises coming solemnly towards him. 'That stocking must certainly be stopped!'

He ran upstairs, and went to Bobbo.

'How can you stop that stocking from sending out any more things?' he asked.

'I don't know,' said Bobbo miserably. 'But perhaps Nancy, the little girl next door, might know. She was one of the good children who were taken to Santa Claus.'

Bobbo's father tore downstairs again, knocking over a duck on the way, and ran to Nancy's house. She was at the front door, watching the things coming out of Bobbo's house, and Bobbo's father told her everything.

'Yes, I think I know how to stop the stocking,' she said. 'Santa Claus told me, in case Bobbo was sorry about his wish. But is he *really* sorry?'

'He certainly is,' said Bobbo's father. 'This has taught us all something, and you may be sure Bobbo won't have a chance to be a horrid, selfish little boy again. He doesn't want to be either.'

Nancy went to Bobbo's house straight away. She picked her way through the animals and came to Bobbo's room, which was full right to the ceiling with toys and pets. The stocking was still performing on a mat near the door, and the little girl pounced on it.

'Where's the ribbon that tied it up?' she asked. 'Oh, there it is!'

She picked up the blue ribbon. Then she held the stocking toe downwards, and shook it violently three times.

At once a strange thing happened. All the toys and animals came rushing towards it, and one by one they took a jump at the stocking, and seemed to disappear inside it. Even the donkey vanished in that way, though Bobbo's father couldn't for the life of him think how. The stocking jerked and jumped as the things disappeared, and very soon the room became quite empty-looking. Still Nancy held the stocking, and then gradually the whole room, stairs and hall were emptied of their toys and animals. All the pets that had wandered into the street came back too, and at last nothing was left at all except the stocking, which lay quiet and still in Nancy's hand.

She took the piece of blue ribbon, and tied it firmly round the mouth of the stocking. Then she gave the stocking to Bobbo's father.

'There you are,' she said. 'It's quite safe now.'

'Thank you, Nancy,' said Bobbo's father gratefully. 'I'll keep it in Bobbo's nursery, just to remind him of what happens to selfish children.'

He carried it in to Bobbo, and told the little boy what Nancy had done.

'Now you'd better make up your mind to turn over a new leaf, and try to be good enough to be chosen properly to go on the trip to Santa Claus's home,' he said.

'I will,' said Bobbo, and he meant it. 'I'll begin this very day, and I'll take my nicest toys to the children in the hospital.'

Bobbo kept his word, and tried his best to be different. He didn't find it easy, but because he had plenty of pluck, he managed it – and you'll be glad to know that the very next Christmas he was awakened one night, and what should he see outside but the reindeer sleigh full of happy laughing children!

'Come on, come on!' cried the elf. 'You really are one of us this time, Bobbo!'

And off they all went with a jingling of bells over the deep white snow!

The Big Girl's
Balloon

The Big Girl's Balloon

ONCE UPON A time a little girl went to a party. It was a birthday party, and there were to be balloons and crackers. Sukie was looking forward to it.

'Now listen, Sukie,' said her mother, as she dressed her for the party. 'There will be a lot of big girls there, I expect, so you must try to be a big girl too, and not cry if you fall down or if you lose your chair at musical chairs.'

'I'll try not to,' said Sukie. 'But, oh Mummy, I hope they don't have a game of tag and catch me! I might cry then!'

'Of course you won't,' said her mother. 'You don't want Geraldine to think you are silly, do you?'

'Oh – is Geraldine going?' said Sukie, pleased. Geraldine was a big girl who lived opposite. Sukie thought she was marvellous. She could ride a bicycle and a horse. She could run faster than anyone else. She had just won a scholarship at school. She went to the same dancing class as Sukie, and she was quite the best there.

'I like Geraldine,' said Sukie. 'She's a very clever girl, I think, Mummy – she's good at everything. And once at the dancing class she chose me for her partner.'

'Well, that was very nice of her,' said Mother, tying Sukie's hair with bright blue ribbons. 'If there is dancing at the party she might choose you again – but she certainly won't if you cry if anything goes wrong.'

'Well, I won't,' said Sukie. 'I promise you, Mummy, that I won't cry if I fall down, and I won't cry if I'm out first at musical chairs, and I won't cry if I'm caught playing tag. I always keep my promises to you, don't I?'

'You do, dear,' said Mother. 'So I know I can trust you not to cry for any of those things. It's not good to cry at somebody's birthday party, anyway – every moment should be happy for the birthday boy or girl.'

Sukie went off to the party. They had tea almost as soon as she got there – and what a lovely tea it was. It began with buns and jam, and ended with the most enormous birthday cake Sukie had ever seen. It had nine candles on it, and little pink roses all round the edge in sugar.

After tea there were games and crackers. Sukie had two crackers and she pulled them with a little boy she knew. She wished Geraldine would pull one with her but she was at the other side of the room.

Geraldine had seen Sukie and smiled at her. She was looking very grand indeed in a deep red velvet frock. Sukie thought she was the nicest girl there.

Geraldine won the musical chairs. As usual, Sukie was the first out, but she didn't cry at all. She stood aside and let the others go on playing, and, to her great delight, Geraldine won the game. She got a most beautiful big red balloon to match her frock.

Sukie thought it was the biggest and best she had ever seen.

After that every boy and girl was given a balloon to play with, but they were very much smaller than Geraldine's prize balloon.

Geraldine hung her red balloon high up on a picture so that it shouldn't pop. She played with her little one, like the others.

Bumping the balloons about all over the place was fun. Sukie had a pretty one. It was like a big green bubble. She liked it very much.

It will be lovely to take it home with me, and hang it in my bedroom, she thought. *I shall look at it in the morning then.*

But a dreadful thing happened almost as soon as she had thought that. Her balloon floated into the air, and came down on top of a sharp ornament on the bookshelf.

Pop! It burst. It was gone. There was nothing left of it but a little bit of dull green rubber.

Sukie was full of horror. Her balloon, her lovely green balloon, had burst. The bang had made her jump – and when she saw that it was her balloon that had popped she was full of dismay.

'My balloon!' she said, and burst into tears.

A grown-up went to see if there were any more balloons left, but there weren't. Sukie sobbed bitterly. And then she saw Geraldine looking at her, and she felt terribly ashamed.

I cried at a birthday party, she thought, and turned away. *In front of Geraldine. Oh, I do feel so ashamed of myself. I promised Mummy I wouldn't cry if I fell down, or was out in musical chairs, or got caught playing tag, but I've cried for something else. And Geraldine will think I'm such a baby. She'll laugh at me. She'll never ask me to dance with her again.*

She went away into a corner to dry her eyes. The others were playing a game of general post. Geraldine was playing it too. But soon Geraldine slipped out of her place and went to Sukie.

'Sukie, come and play,' she said. 'Sukie, look what I've brought you!'

Sukie looked – and looked again. Geraldine was holding out to her her lovely red balloon, the one she had got as a prize.

'Oh, Geraldine, but that's your prize,' said Sukie. 'Oh, I'm sorry I cried. You must have thought I was dreadful.'

'Shall I tell you a secret?' said Geraldine. 'Well, when I was older than you I went to a Christmas party – and my balloon burst too – just like yours. And I cried ever so much louder than you did. So I know just how you feel, you see. And someone was so nice to me – they gave me their balloon. So I thought if ever I had a chance I'd do the same for somebody else.'

'Oh, you are a kind girl,' said Sukie, suddenly feeling very happy. 'But I couldn't take your prize balloon. Did you really cry like me at that Christmas party?'

'Much, much worse,' said Geraldine. 'I had to be taken home, and my mother was so ashamed of me. Now, take my balloon and come and play. And if ever you see somebody crying because their balloon has gone pop, well, you do what I did, and tell them how you cried once, and give them your own balloon!'

'Oh, I will – I will!' said Sukie, and she took the red balloon and went back to play. She felt very happy. Geraldine didn't think she was silly – and she had given her her lovely balloon. She could have danced for joy.

And now, at every party she goes to Sukie is watching for somebody to burst their balloon and cry. She knows what she is going to do then. I'd rather like to do it too, wouldn't you?

Amelia Jane and
the Snow

Amelia Jane and
the Snow

IT WAS SNOWING hard. The toys looked out of the nursery window and watched the big white snowflakes come floating down.

'The garden has a new white carpet,' said the teddy bear.

'Let's send the clockwork clown out to sweep the dust off it!' said Amelia Jane, the big naughty doll, with a giggle.

'Don't be silly, Amelia,' said the clown. 'You do say silly things. There's no dust on a snow carpet!'

'Isn't it pretty!' said the pink rabbit. 'I'd like to go and burrow in it!'

'Let's go and play in it!' said the golden-haired doll. 'It would be such fun.'

'Come on then!' said Amelia Jane. She ran to the door, peeped out, and beckoned the others. 'Nobody's about. We'll slip out of the garden door and go to the bit of garden behind the hedge. Nobody will see us there.'

'Stop a bit, Amelia Jane,' said the clockwork clown. 'Put on a coat. It's very cold outside.'

'Pooh!' said Amelia impatiently. 'Don't be such a baby, clockwork clown! I shall be as warm as toast running about. I'm going!'

She ran off down the stairs. But the other toys stayed to put on hats, coats and scarves. Even the clockwork mouse put a red handkerchief round his neck.

When they got out to the snow they found that Amelia Jane had already made herself a great many snowballs! She danced about as they came, and shouted in glee.

'Let's have a snow fight! Come on! I've got my snowballs ready. Look out, clown! Look out, pink rabbit!'

The big doll threw a snowball hard. It hit the clown on the head and he fell over, plonk! Amelia Jane giggled. She threw a snowball at the golden-haired doll and hit her in her middle. The doll gave a squeal and sat down in the snow.

'Ooh, this is fun!' yelled Amelia. 'Come on, everyone, get some snowballs ready!'

But nobody could make such big hard snowballs as Amelia Jane. Amelia did enjoy herself. She pelted all the toys with snowballs, hitting them on the head and the chest and the legs – anywhere she could. She was quite a good shot, and the toys got very angry.

'Amelia Jane! Stop!' shouted Tom the toy soldier. 'It isn't fair. Your snowballs are three times as big as ours, and you make them so hard that they hurt. Stop, I tell you!'

But Amelia Jane wouldn't stop. No, she went on and on – and how she laughed when all the toys turned and ran away from her shower of snowballs!

'Let's leave her alone,' said the clown crossly. 'She's too tiresome for anything.'

'But she'll follow us and go on snowballing us,' said the mouse.

'No, she won't. She's found something else to snowball,' said the teddy bear. 'Look! She's snowballing the kitten!'

So she was. The kitten didn't mind the snowballs at all because she could always dodge them. She pounced on them as they fell, and Amelia Jane laughed to see her. She forgot about the toys.

'What shall we do?' said the golden-haired doll.

'Let's build a nice, round snow-house,' said the clown eagerly. 'It would be such fun to do that. I know how to. You just pile nice hard snow round in a ring and gradually make a round wall higher and higher. Then you make the wall slope inwards till the sides meet, and that's the roof!'

'Oh, yes, that would be lovely!' said Tom. 'We could all live in the snow-house then.'

'But we won't let Amelia Jane come in at all,' said the clockwork mouse, getting a little snowball for the wall of the house.

'No, we won't,' said the golden-haired doll. 'It will punish her for throwing such hard snowballs at us.'

The toys worked hard at their snow-house. Soon the wall was quite high. It was a perfectly round wall. It grew higher and higher – and at last, as the toys shaped it to go inwards, the round sides met together and made a rounded roof.

The toys made a dear little doorway at the bottom. They were very excited, for the house was lovely. The clown ran to the pond, cut a square piece of ice, and ran back with it.

'What's that for?' asked the pink rabbit.

'A window, of course!' said the clown. He made a square hole in the side of the house and fitted in the piece of ice. It made a lovely window!

'Now let's go inside and be cosy,' said the

golden-haired doll. So they all crowded into the dear little snow-house and sat down. It was lovely.

But just as the clockwork clown was telling a nice story, Amelia Jane came up. The kitten had gone indoors, and Amelia Jane wanted someone else to play with. She had looked and looked for the toys, but as they were in the snow-house she hadn't seen them.

She suddenly saw the house and came running up to it. She peeped inside the window.

'Oh, what a nice little house!' she cried. 'Let me come in too!'

'No, Amelia Jane!' shouted all the toys. 'You are too big. Besides, we don't want you.'

'But I'm very, very cold,' said Amelia Jane, and certainly she was shivering.

'Well, you should have been sensible and put on your coat and hat as we did!' said the golden-haired doll.

'Oh, *do* let me come in!' begged Amelia, who hated to be left out of anything. 'Oh, do let me!'

'NO, NO, NO!' shouted the toys.

'Well, I'm *coming* in!' said Amelia crossly, and she began to push her way in at the door. A bit of the doorway fell down at once.

'Don't!' cried the clown in alarm. 'You will break our house!'

'Serve you right!' said naughty Amelia. But the toys really couldn't bear to see their house broken.

'All right, all right, you can come in,' said Tom. 'But wait till we get out, Amelia. You are so big that there isn't room for anyone else when *you're* inside!'

That pleased Amelia very much. She thought it would be lovely to have the house all to herself. She waited until all the toys had squeezed out of the house, and then she went in.

'Oh, it's lovely!' she cried. She pressed her nose to the window and looked out. 'It's lovely! It's a real little house. This shall be mine. You build another one for yourselves, toys.'

But the toys were tired. They stared angrily at Amelia Jane.

'You are a very naughty, selfish doll,' shouted the teddy bear. 'First you snowball us till we have to run away. Then you take our house for your own.'

'I'm cold,' said the clown, shivering. 'Let's go and slide on the ice for a bit. Perhaps Amelia will get tired of our house soon and we can have it again.'

So they went off to the pond and left Amelia Jane by herself.

Amelia felt cold. She shivered and shook in the little snow-house. 'I wish there was a fire in this house,' she said to herself, 'then it would be nice and warm. I'll make one! How the toys will stare when they see I have a nice fire to warm myself by! But I shan't let them come in at all!'

She ran to the woodshed and got some wood. She found some matches there that the gardener used when he lit a bonfire. She ran back to the snow-house. Soon the twigs were crackling loudly.

'What's that noise?' said the clown suddenly. All the

toys stopped their sliding and listened. It came from their snow-house.

'Amelia Jane is lighting a fire there!' said Tom. Then the toys looked at one another – and began to giggle. They knew quite well what would happen if anyone lit a fire in a house made of snow! They ran up to watch.

'You can't come in, you can't come in!' shouted Amelia Jane. 'This is my house, and this is my own dear little warm fire! Oh, I'm so cosy! Oh, I'm so warm!'

The toys stood and watched. The fire blazed up as the twigs burnt. There was a red glow inside the little house. It certainly looked very cosy. Amelia Jane put out her hands and warmed them inside the house.

But something was happening. The fire was melting the house! After all, it was only made of snow! The walls began to drip. The roof began to drip. The bit of ice that was the window disappeared altogether.

Amelia Jane felt the drips on her back and was cross.

'Who's pouring water on me?' she cried. 'Stop it, or I'll be very angry!'

Drip, drip, drip went the snow as it melted all around her. And suddenly the whole house fell in, for the snow was now so soft and melty that it couldn't hold together. The fire went out with a sizzle.

Amelia Jane disappeared, for the snow fell all over her!

'Oooh! Ow! What's happened?' yelled Amelia Jane, very frightened. She kicked about in the wet snow, and first her hands came out, and then her head. She sat in the snow and looked around.

'Ha, ha! Ho, ho, ho!' roared the toys. 'It serves you right, Amelia Jane! You took our house – and you lit a fire and melted it – and it fell on top of you! Ha, ha! Ho, ho, ho!'

Amelia Jane began to cry. She was wet through and very cold. She ran back to the nursery, leaving little wet marks all the way. She sat by the fire there and tried to get dry.

And very soon she began to sneeze: 'A-tishooo! A-tishoo!'

'Now I've got a cold!' she said miserably. 'Oh, why do I get naughty? Something nasty always happens to me when I do!'

'Well, just try and remember that, next time you feel naughty,' said Tom, giving Amelia his big red handkerchief.

But I don't expect she'll remember it, do you?

The Very Full Stocking

The Very Full Stocking

ONCE UPON A time there was a fat kitten called Fluffy. He lived in a little house with his mother and father, and had a lovely time. They spoilt him dreadfully, because he was their only kitten, so he had all the cream that was on the top of the milk, plenty of sardines and half of his mother's kipper at suppertime.

Now one Christmas night he was very excited. His mother had promised that he should hang up his stocking and that in the morning he would find it filled with all kinds of good things.

'But you must go to sleep quickly, or you will find your stocking empty in the morning,' said his mother.

He went to sleep quickly. He didn't hear the tiny mouse that lived in the hole of the wall come creeping out. He didn't hear the mouse sniffing to see if there were any crumbs on the floor.

The tiny mouse was hungry. The cats didn't leave very much for him to nibble, and he was always terribly afraid of being caught. He came out each night, and sometimes he was lucky enough to find a crumb or two, and sometimes he wasn't.

Tonight he smelt a most delicious smell. It was the smell of cheese, sardines, kipper and lots of other things. Wherever could they be?

The little mouse ran to the end of Fluffy's cot. Good gracious! The smell came from there! The mouse stood up on his back legs and sniffed harder.

What a strange thing! thought the mouse. *Fluffy's stocking is crammed full of delicious things tonight! Never before has there been anything in his stockings – but tonight one of them is quite full. If only I could creep up and have a nibble!*

Well, it didn't take him long to clamber up the bedclothes on to the cot. He ran to where the stocking was hanging on the foot of the cot, and stood up to sniff.

But alas for the poor little mouse! He stood on one of Fluffy's paws! And, of course, that woke up Fluffy at once. Fluffy sat up, wondering who was treading on him – and in a trice he flicked out his paw and caught the trembling mouse!

'Let me go, let me go!' squeaked the mouse in fright.

'What were you doing on my bed?' asked the kitten.

'Only smelling at all the good things in your stocking,' said the mouse. 'That's all. It's a wonderful stocking you have tonight.'

'Is it?' cried Fluffy in surprise, and he too began to sniff. 'Dear me, yes – my stocking is full of the most delicious things to eat. How *dare* you come and sniff at my Christmas stocking, mouse?'

'I'm very sorry,' said the mouse. 'But it's such a marvellous stocking I couldn't help it. Please do let me go.'

'I'll let you go if you can do something impossible,' said Fluffy with a chuckle, for, like all cats, he loved to tease mice.

'What's that?' asked the mouse in fear.

'Well, you see my stocking, don't you?' said the kitten. 'Now, it's quite crammed full – there's not a corner to push in anything else. If you can put something else in my stocking, you may go free! If you can't, I'll eat you for breakfast.'

The little mouse thought hard, his heart beating fast. Then a fine idea came into his tiny head.

'I *can* put in something else,' he said.

'You can't,' said the kitten scornfully. 'Why, not even I could – so I'm sure *you* couldn't.'

'I can,' said the mouse.

'All right. Go on – try,' said the kitten, and he took his paw off the little mouse. The mouse ran to the stocking. He stood up on his hind legs and nibbled away at the bottom of the stocking, at the toe. He nibbled and he nibbled.

'What are you doing?' said the kitten angrily. 'That's not putting anything else in my stocking.'

'Wait,' said the mouse. 'Wait.' And he nibbled again at the toe.

'Mouse, stop nibbling,' cried the kitten. 'You are spoiling my stocking. Unless you tell me at once what you are going to put into it, I'll catch you again!'

'Kitten, use your brains,' said the mouse cheekily. 'I have put something into your stocking that wasn't there before – I have put a hole there! There's always room for a hole, no matter how full a stocking is!'

And without waiting to see what Fluffy would say, the mouse leapt off the cot, ran to his hole and disappeared. Fluffy was angry.

'Putting a hole into my stocking!' he said. 'What next! Bad little mouse! I'll eat him next time I see him!'

But he didn't get the chance, for as soon as Fluffy was fast asleep once more, the mouse came creeping from his hole with two big bags. He went to the end of the cot and, standing on the floor, he waited for the things in the stocking to fall through the hole he had made at the end.

A bit of kipper fell through. That went into the mouse's bag. A whole sardine fell out, and then a piece of cream cheese. Those went into the bags too, and soon they were quite full.

The mouse gave a squeak of delight and ran back to his hole. He put on his new hat, tied a scarf round his neck, for it was a frosty night, and set out to find a new and safer hole, carrying with him enough food to stock a nice big mouse-larder for a week!

I don't know where he went to – but I can't help hoping that such a clever little creature found a good home, and lived happily ever after!

A Week Before
Christmas

A Week Before Christmas

THE JAMESON FAMILY were making their Christmas plans. They sat round the table under the lamp, four of them – Mother, Ronnie, Ellen and Betsy. Daddy was far away across the sea, and wouldn't be home for Christmas.

'Now, we haven't got much money,' said Mother, 'so we must spend it carefully this Christmas. We can't afford a turkey, but I can get a nice fat chicken. I've made a fine big plum-pudding, and I shall buy as much fruit as I can for you. Perhaps I can buy tangerines for a treat!'

'Can we afford a little Christmas tree?' asked Betsy.

She was ten and loved a Christmas tree hung with all kinds of shiny things. 'Just a little one, Mother, if we can't afford a big one.'

'Yes, I'll see what I can do,' said Mother, writing it down on her list. 'And I've made the cake, a nice big one. I've only got to ice it and put Christmassy figures on it. I'll see if I can buy a little red Father Christmas for the middle of it.'

She wrote down, 'Little Father Christmas,' and then wrote something else down below.

'What have you written?' asked Betsy, trying to see. But her mother covered up the words.

'No – I'm writing down what you three want for Christmas! It's not really a secret because you've all told me – and I shall try my hardest to get them.'

Betsy wanted a big doll. She had never had a really big one, though she was ten. She knew she was getting a bit old for dolls now, but she did so love them, and longed to have a big one before she really *was* too old.

Ronnie wanted a box of aeroplane parts so that he

could make a model aeroplane. He had seen one in a shop and longed for it. It would be marvellous to put all the parts together, and at last have a fine model aeroplane that he could take to school and fly for all the boys to see.

Ellen wanted a proper workbasket, one she could keep all her bits of sewing in, and her cottons and scissors and needles too. She was a very good needlewoman for fourteen years old.

'They're all rather expensive presents,' said Ellen to Ronnie and Betsy, when they had discussed what they wanted. 'We mustn't mind if Mother can't get them. But she did say we must tell her what we really wanted. I know what *she* wants – a new handbag. They're expensive too, but if we all put our money together we might be able to buy her the red one we saw the other day – it's thirty shillings.'

So they made their Christmas plans, and discussed everything together. Since their father had been away, Mother had always talked over everything with the children. They knew she hadn't a great deal of money, and they helped her all they could.

'Tomorrow I'm going to go out and do my Christmas shopping,' Mother said. 'I've got to deliver all the parish magazines for the vicar too, because his sister who usually does it is ill. I'll do that first, then I'll go and order the chicken and the fruit and sweets – and perhaps some crackers if they're not too expensive. And I'll see if I can buy your presents too – so nobody must come with me!'

'I'll help with the magazines,' said Ronnie. But Mother shook her head.

'No – you break up tomorrow, and there will be plenty for you to do. You're one of the boys that has promised to go back in the afternoon and help to clean up the school, aren't you?'

'Yes,' said Ronnie. His mother was proud of him because whenever there was a job to be done Ronnie always offered to help. 'But I'll be back in good time for tea, Mother.'

A WEEK BEFORE CHRISTMAS

The girls broke up the next day too. Then there would be six days till Christmas – days to decorate the house with holly from the woods, to make paper chains to go round the walls, to dress the Christmas tree, paint Christmas cards, and do all the jolly things that have to be done before Christmas Day.

'Ellen, you put the kettle on for tea and lay the table, because I shall be a bit late coming back from my shopping this afternoon,' said Mother, the next day, just after dinner. 'I'll try not to be too late – but those magazines take rather a long time to deliver, and I *must* do my shopping afterwards.'

'I'll have tea all ready, Mother,' said Ellen. 'I'll make you some toast!'

Ronnie went off to help at his school. Ellen sat down to draw some Christmas cards. Betsy joined her. The afternoon passed very quickly.

'Do you know, it's snowing very, very hard?' said Ellen suddenly. 'Just look at the enormous flakes falling down, Betsy.'

They got up and went to the window. The ground was already thickly covered with snow. 'Good!' said Betsy. 'Snow for Christmas! That always seems right somehow. And we'll have fun with snowballs and making snowmen.'

'Mother won't like shopping much in this blinding snow,' said Ellen. 'Good thing she's got her rubber boots on. I say, isn't it dark too? I suppose that's the leaden sky. It looks like evening already.'

The snow went on falling all the afternoon. By the time that teatime came it was very thick on the ground. Ronnie came puffing and blowing in from the street, and shook the snow off his coat. 'My word, it's snowy! If it goes on like this we'll be snowed up in the morning!'

Ellen put the kettle on for tea and began to cut some bread and butter. Betsy laid the table. Then she went to the window to look for her mother. But it was dark now and she could see nothing but big snowflakes falling by the window.

'I wish Mother would come,' she said. 'She *is* late. She'll be awfully tired.'

Mother *was* late. The kettle had boiled over two or three times before she came. She opened the front door and came in rather slowly. Betsy rushed to her to help her take off her snowy things. Ellen made the tea.

'Poor Mother! You'll be cold and hungry!' she called. Mother didn't say much. She took off her clothes, put them to dry, and then came in to tea. Ronnie looked at her in surprise. She was usually so cheerful. He saw that she looked sad – and yes, it looked as if she had been crying too! He got up quickly and went to her.

'Mother! What's up? Has anything happened?'

'Yes,' said Mother, and sat down in her chair. 'I've lost my bag – with all my Christmas money in! Oh, children, I've looked and looked for it everywhere, and I can't find it. I must have dropped it when I was taking the big bundle of magazines round.'

The children stared at her in dismay. '*Mother!* All your money in it! Oh, poor darling, what a dreadful shock!'

They all put their arms round her. She tried to smile at them, but their kindness made tears come suddenly into her eyes. She blinked them away.

'It's my own fault. I should have been more careful. I can't think *how* it happened – and now this thick snow has come and hidden everything. I'll never find it!'

The children looked at one another in despair. If the Christmas money was gone, it meant no chicken – no sweets – no fruit – no presents! Not even a Christmas tree!

'You drink a hot cup of tea, Mother, and you'll feel better,' said Ellen. 'What a shame! Never mind, darling, we shan't worry if we don't have quite such a good Christmas!'

'We've got the cake and pudding anyhow,' said Betsy. 'But, oh dear,' she said secretly to herself, 'I shan't have that doll now – and next year I'll be too old to ask for one.' But she didn't say a word of this out loud, of course. She was much too unselfish for that.

'I'll go out and look for your bag tomorrow morning,' said Ronnie.

'The snow will be so thick by then that you wouldn't be able to see anything – even if you knew where to look!' said his mother. 'I don't mind for myself, children – but it's dreadful to think you three won't be able to have anything nice for Christmas – not even the lovely presents I had planned to give you.'

'Don't bother about that,' said Ronnie. '*We* shan't mind. Come on – let's have tea and forget about it.'

But, of course, they couldn't really forget about it. They pretended to talk cheerfully, but inside they all felt miserable. When Mother went in to see Mrs Peters next door, they began to talk about it.

'We shall have to do something about this,' said Ellen. 'Mother will be awfully unhappy if she can't even buy a chicken for Christmas Day. We must make plans!'

'What plans?' asked Betsy.

'Well – to earn a bit of money ourselves. Even if it's

only enough to buy a chicken or a few tangerines, it will be something,' said Ellen.

There was a pause. Then Ronnie spoke suddenly and firmly. 'I know what *I'm* going to do. The chemist's boy is ill and can't deliver medicines for the chemist. I'm going to offer to deliver them till he's better, and he'll pay me a wage. That will be *my* bit of help!'

'Oh, Ronnie – what a very good idea!' said Betsy. 'I wish I could be an errand-girl!'

'You're too small,' said Ronnie. 'You can't do anything. Ellen, can you think of anything *you* can do?'

'Yes, I think so,' said Ellen. 'You know Mrs Harris? Well, she wants somebody to take her three little children for walks each afternoon. I could do that. They're dear little children.'

'Oh, good,' said Ronnie. 'Yes, that would bring in a bit of money too. It's a pity Betsy is too small to do anything. She's not bad for her age.'

Betsy felt sad. She didn't like being the only one who

couldn't earn anything for Christmas. She wondered and wondered what she could do. She even lay awake in bed that night, wondering. And then, just before she fell asleep, she thought of something.

She remembered an old blind lady who lived in the next street. What was her name? Yes, Mrs Sullivan. Mrs Sullivan had a companion who read to her each afternoon. But the companion had gone away for a week's holiday before Christmas. Had Mrs Sullivan got anyone to read to her for that week?

I read quite well, thought Betsy. *I'm the very best in my class. I even read all the hard words without being bothered by them. I shall go tomorrow and ask Mrs Sullivan if she would like me to read to her. Then, if she pays me, I shall be doing my bit too.*

She didn't tell the others, in case they laughed at her. But, next morning after breakfast, she went down the snowy street and found Mrs Sullivan's house.

The snow was now very thick. It had snowed all night long, and in places it was as high as Betsy's knees.

She liked it. It was fun to clamber through the soft white snow. She knocked at Mrs Sullivan's door.

She felt a bit frightened. Mrs Sullivan was rather a fierce-looking old lady and she wore dark glasses that made her look fiercer still. Suppose she was cross that Betsy should dare to come and ask to read to her?

Then Betsy thought of her mother's lost bag with all its money in it. This was one small way of helping. She couldn't turn back now!

Mrs Sullivan's daily woman opened the door and took Betsy into a little room where a bright fire burnt. A big cat sat beside the old lady. The wireless was on, and music flooded the little room. Mrs Sullivan put out her hand, groped round the wireless set, and turned the wireless off.

'Well, it's little Betsy Jameson, isn't it?' she said. 'And what do you want, Betsy?'

'Mrs Sullivan, I heard that your companion is away for a week's holiday,' said Betsy, 'and I didn't know if you'd got anyone to read to you in the afternoons. You see, Mother has lost her bag with all her Christmas money in it, and we're trying to earn a bit to make up – so I thought . . .'

'You thought I might pay you for reading to me, did you?' said Mrs Sullivan. 'Well, I shall have to try you. There's a book somewhere – pick it up and read me a page.'

Betsy found the library book. She began to read in her clear little voice. Mrs Sullivan listened with a smile on her face.

'Yes, you read quite well for your age – ten, aren't you? I shall be pleased to engage you. I will pay you a shilling an hour for reading to me. Come at two o'clock each afternoon, starting today.'

Betsy felt very proud – but a shilling an hour seemed a lot of money just for reading. 'I'd come for sixpence really,' she said. 'I'm not as good as a grown-up at reading.'

'I shall love to have you,' said Mrs Sullivan. 'You won't mind if we don't have reading *all* the time, will you? I mean – it would be nice to talk sometimes, wouldn't it?'

'Oh, yes. But you wouldn't want to pay me just for talking,' said Betsy.

'Well, I'll pay you for your *time*,' said Mrs Sullivan. 'Whether it's reading or talking, or just stroking my cat for me, I'll pay you for keeping me company.'

'Thank you very much,' said Betsy, and she stood up. 'I'll come at two o'clock. I won't be late.'

She went home as fast as ever she could, through the snow. She had something to tell the others! Aha! A whole shilling an hour for six days. If Mrs Sullivan kept her for two hours each afternoon, that would be twelve shillings altogether – enough to buy a chicken, surely!

Ronnie and Ellen thought it was marvellous. They had news to tell too. 'I've got the job at the chemist's,' said Ronnie. 'He asked me a few questions, and rang up my headmaster, and then said I could come till the other boy is well. I've got to deliver medicines from ten to twelve o'clock each morning, and from three to five each afternoon. And he'll tell me if there's anything urgent for the evening.'

'Oh, *good*!' said Ellen. 'Considering you're only twelve, it's jolly fine to get a job as easily as that. You'll have to be careful not to drop any of the bottles.'

'Of course I shall,' said Ronnie rather indignantly. 'How did you get on with *your* job, Ellen?'

'Well, Mrs Harris was very pleased,' said Ellen. 'She's going to pay me half a crown each afternoon for taking all the children out. They're thrilled! I like little children, so I shall enjoy it. Between us we shall get quite a bit of money for Mother.'

'How much is Ronnie earning?' said Betsy.

'Four shillings a day,' said Ronnie. 'Not bad considering it's only a few hours. Four – and Ellen's two-and-six – and Betsy's two shillings – that makes eight-and-six each day to give to Mother. She'll be able to get the chicken and the fruit and the sweets after all.'

'And perhaps a little Christmas tree,' said Betsy hopefully.

The next thing to be done was to tell Mother what they had arranged. How they hoped she wouldn't say they mustn't. Mother listened without a word. Then she spoke in rather a shaky voice.

'Yes, you can all do your little jobs, bless you. I don't think I mind losing my bag when I know what nice children I've got. I'm proud of you all. The money will certainly help to buy the things you'd have to go without, now I've lost my bag.'

Nobody brought Mother's bag back to her. Ronnie thought that people must be very mean indeed not to take a bag back to the person who lost it. He called at the police station twice to ask if anyone had brought it in. But nobody had.

All the children began their jobs that day. Ronnie went off to the chemist, and listened attentively when Mr Hughes told him about the deliveries. 'The addresses are on the wrappings of each bottle or package,' he said. 'Be sure to deliver at the right house, and whatever you do, don't just push any package through the letterbox, in order to be quick.'

Ronnie set off with a basket of bottles and packages. The snow was very thick indeed, and it was a long job taking all the medicines round. Ronnie was astonished at the number of people who were ill. Most of them were very surprised to see him, but when he told them why he was doing it they all smiled and nodded.

'It's a pity more children don't do things like that,' said Mr George. 'Helping their mothers when things go wrong.'

Ellen got on very well too. The three small Harris children were delighted to see her. John, Mike and Sally all tried to cling to her hand at once. She set off very happily with them through the deep white snow.

'We'll play snowballing. We'll build a snowman in the park. I'll try and build you a little snow-house,' promised Ellen. They all had a lovely time, and when she brought them back to their mother at teatime Mrs

Harris exclaimed in delight at their rosy faces and happy talk.

'Oh, Ellen, you've given them such a nice time. Here is your half crown. You'll come again tomorrow, won't you? The children will so look forward to it.'

'I feel sorry you've got to pay me for my afternoon,' said Ellen, feeling quite ashamed of taking the half crown. 'I've had just as good a time as the children, Mrs Harris. I really have.'

'Just wait a minute – I've been baking while you've been out,' said Mrs Harris. 'I've got a cake for you to take home for yourself and that brother and sister of yours – what are their names – Ronnie and Betsy?'

And she gave Ellen a lovely little chocolate cake, wrapped up in paper. Ellen was delighted. How surprised Ronnie and Betsy would be! She thanked Mrs Harris and hurried off home.

She met Betsy at the gate. Betsy's cheeks were red from Mrs Sullivan's bright fire, and from stumbling home through the thick snow. 'Look,' she said, showing

Ellen a bright two-shilling piece. 'That's my first wage. And isn't it strange, Ellen, Mrs Sullivan likes just the kind of stories *I* like! We read a most exciting school story for a whole hour!'

Mother smiled at all the cheerful talk. She had got hot toast and butter and honey ready, and the chocolate cake was put in a place of honour on the table. The children sat down hungrily.

'And Mrs Sullivan and I talked a lot,' said Betsy. 'She told me all about when she was a girl – oh, ever so long ago – and I told her about Ronnie and Ellen and you, Mother. And then I had to brush the cat, Jimmy, and change his ribbon and get him some milk. I really did have a very nice time. I can hardly wait till tomorrow to find out what happens in the story I'm reading to Mrs Sullivan.'

'I bet she chose a story like that because you wouldn't be able to read a grown-up one,' said Ronnie.

'She didn't! She laughed at all the funny bits too,' said Betsy. 'There's a mam'zelle in the book and the girls are always playing tricks on her. We laughed like anything.'

'Mrs Sullivan is very kind,' said Mother. 'Very, very kind. I ought to pay *her* for having you like this.'

'Oh, no, Mother – it's a job of work, really it is,' said Betsy earnestly. 'Mrs Sullivan says it's not easy to be a really good companion, and she says I am. Really she does.'

'You're a lovely little companion,' said Mother. 'Mrs Sullivan is lucky to have you. But I think she knows it. Well, as I have said before – what nice children I have got!'

'Well, we've got a jolly nice mother,' said Ronnie unexpectedly. 'And what's more, Mother, I once heard the headmaster's wife saying to the head that she had noticed that all the nicest children were the ones that had the best mothers – so, if you think *we're* nice, you've got yourself to thank!'

Everybody laughed. They all felt happy and cosy. It was so nice to help, and to do a job well. Really it didn't seem to matter any more that Mother had lost her bag!

All the children went to their jobs each day, cheerfully and willingly. Mr Hughes the chemist, Mrs Harris and blind Mrs Sullivan welcomed them and wished there were more children like them. Ronnie broke no bottles, Ellen made the three Harris children happy, and as for Betsy it would be hard to know which of the two, she or Mrs Sullivan, enjoyed themselves the more.

'Jimmy always purrs loudly when he sees me coming,' Betsy said. 'I wish I had a kitten. Jimmy purrs like a boiling kettle. I put a green ribbon on today and it matched his eyes. It's a pity Mrs Sullivan can't see how nice he looks.'

By the time that the day before Christmas came the children had got their mother quite a lot of money. Enough to buy the chicken, the fruit and a box of crackers! Marvellous!

Just as Ronnie was going home on Christmas Eve

morning to get dinner, Mrs Toms called him. She lived in a little house in the middle of the village and she was a friend of his mother's.

'Ronnie! Would you have time to sweep away the snow for me before you go to the chemist's this afternoon? I did ask a man to come and do it but he hasn't turned up, and I've got my sister and her children coming on Christmas Day tomorrow. I know you're earning money for your mother and I'd be very glad to pay you for the sweeping.'

'No, I'll do it for nothing,' said Ronnie. 'I'd like to. It would be nice to do something for nothing for a change, Mrs Toms. Have you a broom and a spade? If you have I'll come along at two o'clock this afternoon, before I go to Mr Hughes, and clean up your front path for you.'

'You're a kind child,' said Mrs Toms. 'Thank you very much. If you won't let me pay you, I shall give you some of our apples and pears for Christmas instead. I had a lot from my garden this year, and I've saved plenty. So you shall have a basketful to take home.'

Christmas was going to be good after all, thought Ronnie as he went home. He was out again just before two and went to Mrs Toms's house. A spade and broom were waiting for him outside the front door. Ronnie took the spade first. How thick and deep the snow was! Except for a little path, it had been untouched for days, and was quite deep.

He began to dig, shovelling the snow away to the side. He worked hard, and soon took off his coat, he felt so hot.

When he got almost up to the front door he dug his shovel into the snow, and threw aside a great heap. As the snow fell, something dark showed in it. It tumbled to the side with the snow. Ronnie glanced at it.

Then he looked again, more carefully. He dropped his spade and picked up the dark package. It was a brown bag!

'Mrs Toms! I've found Mother's bag!' yelled Ronnie

suddenly, making Mrs Toms almost jump out of her skin. 'Look, it's Mother's bag – buried in the snow outside your front door!'

Mrs Toms came hurrying out. 'My goodness, is it really her bag? Yes, it is. She must have dropped it in the snow when she came delivering magazines some days ago. Would you believe it! And now you've found it! Well, well – what a good thing you're a kind-hearted lad, and came to sweep my snow away for me – or someone else might have found it and stolen it, when the snow melted!'

'I'll just finish this,' said Ronnie joyfully, 'then maybe I'll have time to rush home and tell Mother before I start delivering medicines. Oh, my word – what a find, I can hardly believe it!'

He rushed home with the bag. Ellen and Betsy were not there; they had gone to their jobs. But Mother was there, and she stared in delight when Ronnie held out the wet bag.

'*Ronnie!* Oh, Ronnie, where *did* you find it? Is my

money in it? Oh yes, everything's there, quite safe. Oh, Ronnie, this is wonderful. Just in time for Christmas too! I shall go shopping this very afternoon, because now I shall be able to buy you all the presents. I thought you would have to go without. It's too good to be true!'

It was a very happy and joyful Christmas for the Jameson family that year. There was plenty to eat after all, and as much fruit and chocolate and sweets as anyone wanted. There was a Christmas tree hung with all kinds of things and topped with a lovely Father Christmas sent home with Betsy from Mrs Sullivan. Mrs Toms sent a basket of apples and pears. Mrs Harris gave Ellen a big box of chocolates for everyone. And Mr Hughes presented Ronnie with a box of sweet-scented soap for his mother.

'Everybody's so kind,' said Ellen happily. 'Oh, Mother – this is the loveliest workbasket you've given me. It's as good as a grown-up's one.'

'And my model aeroplane set is *much* better than I

expected,' said Ronnie. 'Mother, you've bought me a more expensive one than I said – it'll make a much bigger aeroplane.'

'I shall call my doll Angela Rosemary Caroline Jameson,' said Betsy, hugging an enormous doll. 'She's the biggest doll I've ever seen and the nicest. Oh, Mother – we never thought Christmas would be like this, did we, when you lost your bag?'

'No,' said Mother, who was busy putting all her things from her old handbag into her new red one. 'We didn't. I didn't think I'd have this lovely bag, for instance. I didn't think I'd be able to get all the things you wanted, or any nice things to eat. But you've managed it between you. I'm proud of you. There aren't many children who would do what *you* have done!'

But *you* would, wouldn't you? It's marvellous how a bit of bad luck can be changed into something good if everybody helps!

The Cracker
Fairies

The Cracker
Fairies

ELSIE AND WILLIAM were so unhappy that they cried streams of tears down their cheeks – and, indeed, it wasn't surprising because they both had bad colds on Christmas Day, and had to stay in bed!

'It *is* bad luck!' said Mummy. 'But it's just no good letting you get up – you might be really ill. So you must play with your presents in bed, and try and be happy.'

But poor Elsie and Will found it very difficult to be happy. Their new toys were on their beds, but they didn't feel like playing with them. They could wind up their new train and new motorcars and bus, but they couldn't let them run on the bed – they got caught in the sheets! So it really wasn't any fun at all.

Mummy was so busy too, because Grannie and Grandpa, Auntie Ellen and Uncle Jim and their children were all coming to tea that afternoon. She had such a lot of things to get ready that she really hadn't had much time for Elsie and William.

'Could John, Joan and Jessie come to see us this afternoon when they come?' asked Elsie.

Mummy shook her head. 'No,' she said. 'You might give them your cold and that would never do. I'm so sorry, darlings, but we will give you a treat when you are better – and you must just be as cheerful as you can without any visitors to see you today.'

Now it so happened that twelve little fairies came by that way, and peeped in at the children's window. When they saw Elsie and William crying they were most surprised.

'Look at that!' said the biggest fairy. 'Crying on Christmas Day! Whatever's happened? Do you suppose they didn't get any presents?'

floor for you to see, if you like,' said the biggest fairy. So down they all flew, and soon the engine, the motorcars and the bus were running busily over the floor. Then the second fairy, who was very good at reading, read a whole story to the children from one of the new books.

By that time it was dinnertime and the children's mother came in with their dinner. The fairies hid under the pillows at once. Mummy was *most* surprised to see the children looking so happy and cheerful!

When they ate their dinner the twelve fairies sat round the edges of the two plates and nibbled crumbs of bread. It was so funny to see them. When Mummy came in again they slipped under the sheet. Elsie nearly laughed out loud because one fairy tickled her leg!

'Now you must have your rest,' said Mummy, and she tucked them up. As soon as she had gone, the fairies slipped out from the bed. 'Where can we have a rest too?' they asked.

'Could you all get into my doll's cot, do you think?' asked Elsie.

They flew over to it. They scrambled in, put their tiny heads on the pillow and were soon just as fast asleep as the two children.

They had tea with the children when they woke up, and when Mummy brought Elsie and William two balloons the fairies played with them all over the room. They flew in the air and bumped the balloons up to the ceiling.

'You are so funny!' laughed Elsie. 'I've never seen anyone play with balloons like that before!'

Then it was time for the fairies to go. They kissed the children, and do you know what two of the fairies gave them – a tiny silver wand each that would do magic!

Mummy found the wands under the pillow. 'I suppose these little things came out of the crackers?' she said. 'What dear little toys!'

'They *did* come out of the crackers!' Elsie whispered to Will. 'They came with the Cracker Fairies!'

The Dog That
Hated Christmas

The Dog That Hated Christmas

THERE WAS ONCE a dog who hated Christmas. Now this may seem strange to you, who think Christmas is the jolliest time of the year – but, you see, Rollo, this dog, lived with a dull family who always went away at Christmas time to a hotel.

And the hotel wouldn't take dogs. So poor Rollo was always left behind in the house with the old rather bad-tempered cook. She didn't like Rollo, so she shut him up in an attic with a dish of dry biscuits and a bowl of water all alone. There he stayed, forlorn and miserable, until his family came back.

It was no wonder that he hated Christmas, was it?

As soon as he heard the word, he began to shiver and shake, for nobody but a dog knows how lonely a feeling it is to be shut up all day long and never see a kind face or hear a kind word.

Now there came a time when Rollo's family wanted to move away to another country altogether, and they didn't want to take Rollo. So they gave him to the gardener, who took him home to his cottage and showed him to his children.

There had been no children in Rollo's family, and at first the dog was half scared of the merry shouts and hearty pats he got. But soon he loved it all and made friends with John the boy, Alice the girl and Pip the baby. He loved the children's mother too; she was so kind and merry.

'Rollo! Rollo! Where are you?' shouted the children all day long. 'Come for a walk. Come for a game. Come for your dinner. Rollo! Rollo!'

And Rollo always scampered up, woofing loudly, his tail wagging as fast as a propeller of an aeroplane. He was as happy as the day is long, and he couldn't help hoping that his first family would not want him back again.

Then one day he heard the word he hated.

'Christmas will soon be here,' said John.

'Oooh, Christmas!' said Alice.

'Ooh!' said the baby, who had only had one Christmas, but thought it must be something lovely.

Rollo put his tail down when he heard the word 'Christmas'. He crept into a corner.

'Gracious! What's the matter with Rollo?' said Alice in surprise. 'Are you ill, Rollo? Have you been naughty? Why do you look so sad and miserable?'

Rollo put his head on his paws and looked at the three children. 'Woof, woof, woof, woof!' he said. That meant, 'Who wouldn't be miserable when Christmas comes? Horrid time of year.' But the children didn't understand at all.

Nearer and nearer Christmas came. Every time Rollo heard people talking about it he shivered and trembled, and thought of being shut up for days alone. And he suddenly made up his mind to run away for Christmas.

Yes, he would run right away, and then nobody could go and leave him shut up in a nasty, musty room without a kind word or pat. He would go to a farm he knew and live in a stable till that horrid Christmas time was over.

So, on Christmas Eve, Rollo crept out of the back door and ran off to the farm nearby. He snuggled himself down in the stable straw, put his head on his paws and thought how he hated Christmas. He didn't think he would find anything to eat for a few days, unless the horses let him share their corn – but never mind, he would have a good meal when he went back.

Rollo slept peacefully on the straw, while the big carthorses snorted and breathed their steamy breath into the air. He awoke early on Christmas morning and remembered where he was. Good! Nobody had shut him up alone *this* Christmas. But, tails and whiskers, how hungry he was!

A horse gave him a few grains of corn. While Rollo was chewing them, a big black cat poked her nose in at the door.

'Oh, there you are, Rollo,' she said. 'Why have you left your nice family? The children are crying because they can't find you.'

'Haven't the family gone away then?' asked Rollo in surprise. 'My first family always did.'

'Of course they haven't,' said the cat. 'Families don't always do the same things. You'd better go back.'

'But if I do, I shall be locked up alone for days,' said Rollo. 'I know all about Christmas, black cat. I've seen five Christmases and they were all as horrid as each other.'

'Well, do as you please,' said the cat, and walked off, her long tail straight up in the air.

Rollo lay and thought for a while, and then he made up his mind that he couldn't bear to think of those children crying for him – he would go back, even if they *did* lock him up for Christmas. So he ran out of the stable and scampered home down the frosty white roads.

The door was shut. He scraped at it with a paw. John opened it – and he gave a great shout.

'Rollo! Dear, dear Rollo! We thought you were lost for ever. Happy Christmas, Rollo.'

He hugged the surprised dog, and then Alice patted him hard, crying, 'Happy Christmas, Rollo darling. Where have you been? We were so miserable without you – but now Christmas will be lovely.'

'Lovely,' said the baby, crawling to Rollo and hanging on to his tail.

'Rollo, here's your Christmas present,' said John, and he gave Rollo the very biggest, juiciest bone he had ever seen.

'And here's what *I've* bought you,' said Alice, and she gave him a bag of his favourite biscuits. 'I bought them with my own money for you because I love you. You are the dearest dog in the world.'

'Woof! Woof!' said Rollo, and he wanted to cry because he was so surprised and happy.

Then Pip the baby stroked Rollo and gave him a red ball. 'Ball,' said Pip. 'Ball.'

Bones and biscuits, thought the happy dog. *What sort of a Christmas is this? Aren't they going to lock me up alone?*

'Good dog, Rollo,' said the children's mother, and she held out a grand new collar for his neck. 'This is for a good dog. See if it fits him, John.'

It did – and Rollo did look fine. Then the children's father tied a red ribbon to the collar to make Rollo look Christmassy.

'Woof!' said Rollo, wishing he could show himself to the black cat. 'Happy Christmas, everybody. So this is what Christmas is really like – all kindness and love. Ah, I'll never say I hate it again.'

That afternoon he took a few biscuits to the horse who had shared his corn with him.

'Happy Christmas,' he said to the horse. 'Did you know it was Christmas? Christmas is a lovely time.'

'Ah, you've changed your mind,' said the horse, munching the biscuit. 'Christmas is what people make it, Rollo. Just you tell everybody that, and it will be a wonderful time for grown-ups and children and animals too.'

So Rollo sends you a message, children. He says, 'Make others happy at Christmas and you'll be happy yourself too.'

The Goblin Who
Stole Sweets

The Goblin Who
Stole Sweets

SOMEBODY WAS STEALING sweets out of the toy sweetshop in the nursery! There were twelve bottles of sweets there – and every day some of them disappeared.

'*I'm* not stealing them!' said Teddy bear.

'And I wouldn't touch *one*,' said the sailor doll, though he was very fond of sweets.

'Well, someone's stealing them,' said the doll. 'And what Janet and Ronnie will say when they find out that their toyshop sweets are gone, I really can't think!'

'We must find out who is taking them,' said the blue rabbit. 'They disappear in the afternoons, when the children are out for their walk and we are shut up in the toy cupboard.'

'Well, this afternoon we will take the key of the cupboard away, so that Nanny can't lock the door!' said Teddy. 'Then we'll creep out and see who is the thief.'

So that afternoon, when Janet and Ronnie had gone out for a walk, and had left the toys in the cupboard, they all crept out and hid in different places in the nursery, so that they might watch for the robber.

The sailor doll sat up on the nursery windowsill behind the curtain. He looked out of the window.

'Ooooh!' he said. 'It's snowing! There is a white carpet all over the ground. I can see all the way down the hill, and there's snow everywhere. I wish we could toboggan!'

'Sh!' said the blue rabbit. 'Somebody is coming!'

And sure enough somebody was! It was a little green goblin with naughty eyes. He slipped in at the door, and ran to the toy sweetshop. In a trice he picked up two of the bottles of sweets, and was just going to uncork them when the sailor doll shouted at him.

'Stop, thief! You naughty robber! Put down those bottles at once!'

The goblin jumped. He looked round – but when he saw only toys watching him, he grinned.

'Shan't!' he said.

'You jolly well will!' said the teddy, and he rushed at the goblin. But quick as lightning the little green fellow ran to the door and out. He slipped into the garden and ran to the gate. Then, staggering about in the thick snow, he began to go down the white hillside with the two bottles of sweets.

'He's taken two whole bottles!' said Teddy.

'Stop him!' said the blue rabbit.

'How?' asked the doll, very worried.

'Come on, I'll show you!' yelled the sailor doll suddenly, and with one leap he was down from the windowsill. He caught up the tin nursery tray and rushed outside, followed by all the rest of the toys.

They ran to the gate quite easily, for the snow had been swept away from the path.

'But how can we get down this snowy hill?' asked the doll in dismay.

'That's what I brought the tray for – to get down the hill before the goblin does!' cried the sailor doll, and he slammed the tray on the snow at the top of the hill. 'Get on, everyone.'

They all got on, though the blue rabbit was very much afraid. The sailor doll gave the tin tray a push and leapt on at the back. The tray slid down the hill.

Whoooooooosh! What a slide that was! The tray sped on over the snow like a toboggan, and carried all the toys with it. My word, what a pace it went! You should have seen it! The blue rabbit's whiskers were almost blown off.

The green goblin was still staggering down the hill, deep in the snow. The tray sped after him.

'Whoooooooosh!' cried all the toys. 'Look out!'

The goblin heard the noise and looked behind him.

He gave a yell. The tray was almost on top of him. He tried to jump out of the way, but it wasn't any good.

Bang! The tray hit him in the back and sent him deep into the snow. He disappeared into the whiteness, and all the toys fell off the tray.

'Ooooh!' said the sailor doll.

'I've bent my whiskers,' said the blue rabbit.

'Where are those bottles of sweets?' cried the bear. 'Oh – here's one.'

'And here's another!' shouted the doll, picking the second one up from the snow.

'But where's the goblin?' asked the sailor doll.

'We'd better dig him out,' said the rabbit.

'Look! There are the children coming home from their walk!' cried Teddy. 'We must get home quickly before they see us. Never mind the goblin!'

They all scrambled back up the hill, and in at the nursery door. They shook the snow off themselves as best as they could, stood the tray in the corner, and scurried into the cupboard – only just in time!

'I can't think why our toys feel so wet,' said Janet, when she opened the cupboard and took them out. 'I'd very much like to know what they've been doing!'

Well, if she asked the green goblin, she'd soon know what the toys had been up to. But, dear me, the green goblin was at the bottom of the snow! And there I'm afraid he'll have to stay till it melts. Serves him right, the naughty little thing!

The Christmas
Tree Party

The Christmas
Tree Party

THE CHILDREN ACROSS the road were going to have a party. Janey knew, because she had seen an enormous Christmas tree arriving there, and she had seen a most beautiful Christmas cake being taken in too, with candles all round it!

Janey wished she knew the children across the road, but she didn't. Janey didn't go to their school, and their mother wouldn't let them play with children they didn't know. So Janey just had to watch them and wonder about them – but she did wish she knew them, and could play games with them and go to their lovely, lovely parties!

'Mummy!' she said. 'Look! The children across the

road are going to have a party. I can see somebody putting lights and ornaments on the Christmas tree in the front room.'

'Horrid, stuck-up children!' said Janey's brother. 'They think themselves too good for us! I hope they have a horrid party!'

'Don't be unkind, Robin,' said Mother. 'They look very nice children to me.'

'I'm going to watch what happens,' said Janey. 'If only they don't draw their curtains I can see everything plainly. I believe they are going to have tea in the front room too – I can see someone putting a big white cloth over a long table.'

Janey watched for a long time. It did seem as if the party was going to be a beautiful one! Janey counted how many chairs were round the table – sixteen! Plates of sandwiches and cakes and buns and bowls of jellies and trifles. And right in the very middle of the table was the big Christmas cake, but the candles would not be lit until teatime.

'A Christmas tree party is the very best kind of party,' said Janey to herself. 'Oh, I do believe the children's mother is going to put all the presents on the tree now!'

So she was! The tree reached almost to the ceiling, and already had dozens of lights on it, and some bright, shiny ornaments and coloured balls. Now the mother was hanging dolls and engines and books and motorcars and all kinds of exciting toys on it. Janey felt so excited herself that she had to jump up and down on the chair she was kneeling on!

'Anyone would think you were going to the party yourself!' said Robin grumpily. 'Can't you keep still?'

'No, I can't,' said Janey. 'It's all so exciting. Do come and watch, Robin.'

'No, thank you,' said Robin. 'If I can't go to a party I don't want to watch other people going to it!'

'They're arriving!' cried Janey. 'Here's a car with two little girls in it. One has a blue party frock and the other has a yellow one, and they both have ribbons in their hair and blue capes. And here come two boys walking down the street with their father. And here's another car – with three children and their mother. Oh, how excited they must feel!'

Janey watched all the children run up the path and go into the house. She hoped they would go into the front room, but they didn't.

'They must be playing games before tea in the room at the back,' she told Robin. 'What fun it will be to watch them come and have tea!'

There was very little to see after that, for no one came into the front room at all. The tea was ready, and the Christmas tree was waiting with its lights twinkling. Everyone was playing musical chairs with the children in the back room.

Janey sat and looked at the house opposite, loving the firelight that shone over the tea table, and trying to see all the presents that hung on the big Christmas tree.

And then she noticed a very peculiar thing. The Christmas tree seemed to be falling over a bit. Yes – it was certainly slanting forward. How strange!

Janey watched, half scared. The tree tilted over a little more – it seemed to be falling towards the tea table. It would spoil all the cakes and the jellies – it would crush that beautiful Christmas cake! It must be too heavy for its tub. It was slowly falling, falling over!

'Robin! Look!' cried Janey. 'The Christmas tree is falling over! Everything will be spoilt!'

'And a good thing too,' said unkind Robin, who hated to see anyone having things he hadn't got. 'Let it fall and break everything up!'

'Oh no, no, no!' cried Janey. 'Oh no! It is too beautiful to be spoilt, and the children will be so unhappy! I shall go and tell them!'

And before Robin could say a word more the little girl shot out of the room, out of the front door and across the street! She banged at the door there and when the mother came to open it in surprise, Janey told her why she had come.

'Your Christmas tree is falling down!' she cried. 'It's spoiling itself and the lovely tea table! I saw it from my window. Oh, quick, come and stop it!'

She and the mother ran into the front room and were just in time to save the big Christmas tree from toppling over altogether! Nothing had been spoilt – but Janey was only just in time! The father came running in, and very soon he had the tree upright again, safely packed in its tub, and weighted down with some big stones.

'Well!' said the mother, looking at Janey. 'What a lucky thing it was for us that you were watching the tree! Thank you so much.'

'I've been watching everything,' said Janey. 'It was so exciting – seeing all the table laid with those lovely things – and watching the children come – and seeing you hang the presents on the tree. It was almost as good as coming myself. I'm glad I saved the tree for you.'

'Are you the little girl that lives over the road?' asked the mother. 'My children have often said they would like to know you. Let's run across the road to your mother and see if she will let you come to the party! One little girl hasn't come because she has a cold, so we have an empty place. It would be so nice if you could come!'

Well, think of that! Janey could hardly believe her ears! She took the mother's hand and they ran across the road. In a few minutes Janey's mother had heard all about how Janey had saved the Christmas tree from falling on to the tea table, and Janey was putting on her pink party frock and brushing her hair in the greatest excitement!

Robin stood and watched. How he wished he had been as kind as Janey! If only he had run across with her and saved the tree, perhaps he would have been asked too. But he had been jealous and sulky – and that never brings treats or surprises, as kindness does!

Janey went to the party, and oh, what a fine one it

was! All the children were told how Janey had saved the party and they thought she was wonderful.

And what do you think Janey had from the Christmas tree? Guess! She had the beautiful fairy doll off the very top, because everyone said she ought to have the nicest present of all. Wasn't she lucky? But she really did deserve that doll, didn't she?

Now she is great friends with the children across the road, and so is Robin. They play together every Saturday and go to tea once a week. It was a good thing that Janey watched the party that afternoon, wasn't it?

The Little
Christmas Tree

The Little
Christmas Tree

IT WAS BITTER weather. The frost stayed on the grass all day long, and the ground was as hard as iron – too hard for even the blackbird's strong orange beak to break when he looked for worms. There were no insects for the robin and the wren. The little birds shivered when they went to roost, for even the thick ivy let in the cold, frosty wind at night. They were cold and hungry – yes, and thirsty too, for the frost had turned every pond and puddle into ice.

'It's Christmas time, Christmas time!' sang the thrush, who couldn't help singing even when he was cold and hungry. 'But there are no presents for us little birds! Nothing to eat – nothing to drink! We shall starve and freeze, and nobody cares!'

The day before Christmas was bitterly cold, and the birds could find no food anywhere except for a few crumbs that a small girl threw out of her window – but they didn't go very far among a hundred hungry beaks!

'Tomorrow I shall die of hunger!' carolled the robin in despair.

'And I shall die of thirst!' said the wren in his loud voice.

But the next morning, Christmas Day, what a surprise for the birds! Out of one of the houses nearby came two small children, carefully carrying a little Christmas tree! They set it on the stump of an old tree and left it there for the birds to see.

The tree was hung with tinsel and jolly glass ornaments – but with lots of other things as well! Bits of bacon rind were tied to the branches, and pieces of coconut. Crusts of bread and biscuits hung there too, and two big bones. Strings of unshelled peanuts were draped round and round the little tree, and, stuck on to the spiky branch at the top, was half a coconut, white and sweet. Packed into the pot in which the tree stood was a mixture of dripping and seed, lying firmly on top of the earth.

'Look! Look! A Christmas tree for us!' cried the thrush in excitement.

'Be careful it is not a trap,' said the wily blackbird, who was always on the lookout for cats, traps and snares.

'I will fly down and see,' said the robin, who was bold and friendly, and always believed that children would be kind. So down he flew and perched on a branch. Soon he was pecking away at a biscuit, and singing joyfully, 'It's a tree for us, for us, for us! Trilla, trilla, come and see, it's such a lovely Christmas tree!'

Down flew a dozen sparrows, and found the seeds at the bottom and the bread on the branches. Then came the blue tits, the coal tits and the great tits, to feast on the coconut, the fat and the peanuts. Six noisy starlings flew down afterwards, and squabbled loudly over the two bones and the bacon rind. The thrush came with his brother and two blackbirds. The wren flew down, and three pretty chaffinches joined him, to peck up the seed in the pot.

The two children watched from the window. They were full of delight to see so many birds on their little tree.

'This is the biggest treat we've had this Christmas!' they said to one another. 'What fun!'

'And this is the biggest treat we've EVER had!' sang the bright-eyed robin. 'A merry Christmas to you both! We'll fill your garden with song in the springtime!'

I'd love to hear them, wouldn't you!

What Happened
on Christmas Eve

What Happened on Christmas Eve

'NOW – ARE we all ready?' asked Santa Claus, standing by his reindeer sleigh. 'Sack in? All the toys in it that I asked for – especially those new aeroplanes for the boys? Have the reindeer had a good feed?'

'Yes, sir,' said his little servant. 'Look at them stamping their feet and tossing their antlers in the air! They are longing to go. Goodbye, sir. I hope you have a good journey. You will find you have plenty of toys in the sack, and you know the spell to use if you want some more.'

'Right,' said Santa Claus and stepped into his sleigh. 'Brrrrr! It's a cold and frosty night. Pull the rug closely round my feet, please.'

He was well tucked in. He took the reins and clicked to the four impatient reindeer. 'Get along then! Up into the air with you – and for goodness' sake look out for telegraph wires before you land on anyone's roof!'

Bells began to ring very loudly as the reindeer galloped over the snow and then rose smoothly in the air, their feet still galloping. Only reindeer belonging to Santa Claus could gallop through the air. They loved that. It was a wonderful feeling.

They soon left the sky over Toyland and galloped into the sky over our land. The moon sailed up and lit everything. Santa Claus peered downwards.

'We're there! Go a bit lower, reindeer, I must just look at my notebook to see the names there.'

'Peter Jones, Sara White, Ben White, Michael Andrews . . . they all live somewhere here. Land on a roof nearby, reindeer.'

The reindeer galloped downwards. The biggest one looked out for telegraph wires. The year before he had caught his hooves in some and had nearly upset the sleigh. He guided the others safely down to a big roof, where a large chimney stood.

Santa Claus got out and pulled his sack from the sleigh. 'Two children here,' he said. 'Sara and Ben White. Good children too. I shall leave them some nice toys.'

He disappeared down the chimney. The reindeer waited patiently. One of them began to paw at the roof, and then stopped quickly. He remembered that he had been told never to do that. It might wake up the children of the house if they heard someone knocking on the roof!

The breath of the reindeer looked like steam in the frosty, moonlit air. They stood and stared out over the quiet town. This was a big adventure for them, and they enjoyed every minute of it.

Santa Claus popped his head out of the chimney. 'Give me a pull,' he said to the biggest reindeer.

The reindeer turned his big head and put his mouth down to Santa Claus's neck. He tugged at the back of his cloak there, and Santa Claus came up with a jerk, his sack after him.

'Thanks,' he said. 'I must have got a bit bigger. I never got stuck in that chimney before. The two children were fast asleep, reindeer. They *have* grown since last year. The girl has stopped biting her nails. I noticed that. I gave her a specially nice doll because I felt so pleased.'

'Hrrrrumph,' said the reindeer, sounding pleased too. In a minute or two they were all galloping off at top speed again, the bells jingling.

Santa Claus was very busy. He left toys here, there and everywhere. Then he came to a little village and peered downwards. 'There are two children somewhere down there,' he said. 'Let me see – what were their names? Ah, yes – Elizabeth and Jonathan. Now – where's my notebook? What shall I leave them this year?'

He turned the pages and looked down a list of names. 'Oh, dear! The report I had of them this year isn't good. They've been rude to their mother – and have been lazy at school. I'm afraid I can't leave them anything. And they did seem such nice children last year. What a pity! Reindeer – go on to the next big town, please. There are a lot of children there.'

And then something happened. An aeroplane came flying by, fairly low, just as the reindeer galloped upwards into the frosty sky. There wasn't a collision because the biggest reindeer swerved at once – but the aeroplane caused such a tremendous current of air, as it passed close to the sleigh, that Santa Claus felt himself being blown off! He clutched at the side of the sleigh and just managed to hold on, though his legs were blown over the side and he had to climb back very carefully indeed.

He sat down and mopped his forehead. 'My word! What a narrow escape!' he said. 'I feel quite faint. Go slowly to the next town, reindeer. I've had a fright.'

So they went very slowly indeed, and Santa Claus lay back in his rugs and got over the shock. He didn't know that his sack of toys had been blown right out of the sleigh!

It had risen in the air when the aeroplane almost bumped into them, and had then dropped downwards. It landed with a tremendous thud on the roof of a house, burst open, and flung all the toys inside to the ground. They rolled down the roof one by one – ships, dolls, balls, teddy bears, trains and all.

Bumpity-bump! Clitter-clat! Rillobyroll! Down they went and fell all over the garden below.

The two children in the house were wide awake. They hadn't been to sleep at all. They were Elizabeth and Jonathan Frost, the two children that Santa Claus was not going to give any toys to because their school reports had been bad, and because they had been so rude to their mother that year.

They hadn't been able to go to sleep because they were unhappy. Their mother was ill in hospital – just at Christmas time! Nothing could be worse.

'I wouldn't feel so bad about it if only we hadn't been

so horrid to Mother,' said Jonathan. 'She never said a word about being ill – and we kept on being rude. Whatever came over us to be so horrid?'

'I don't know,' said Elizabeth. 'And now we've upset Daddy too, because our bad school reports came on the very day Mother went to hospital – just as if he hadn't already had too much bad luck. I feel awful. I wish we'd had good reports to cheer up poor Daddy.'

'There won't be any presents this Christmas,' said Jonathan gloomily. 'Mother away – Daddy upset. Nobody will think about us at all.'

'Well, Mrs Brown next door said it served us right to have a miserable Christmas,' said Elizabeth. 'She said she'd heard us being cheeky to Mother. And she said if we hadn't been so horrid to poor Mother, she would have bought us presents herself, but she didn't think we deserved any.'

'Well, we don't,' said Jonathan. 'We've been simply ... I say! What's that noise? It sounds like bells!'

It *was* bells. The children listened. Then they heard

another sound. 'An aeroplane!' said Elizabeth. 'Isn't it low? I wonder what those bells were.'

Suddenly there was a tremendous thud on the roof. Crash! Then came lots of other, smaller noises. *Bumpity-bump! Clitter-clat! Rilloby-roll!*

The children sat up straight and looked out of the window. In the moonlight they saw a lot of little dark things falling. Whatever was happening?

'What is it?' said Jonathan, scared. 'Something fell on the roof. Do you think it was something the aeroplane dropped? Shall we go and look?'

'Yes,' said Elizabeth, scrambling out of bed. She dragged on her thick robe and put on warm slippers. 'Quick! Come and see.'

They went down the stairs and opened the back door. Scattered all over the garden were many little dark things. Elizabeth picked up the first one and looked at it in the moonlight.

'Jonathan! It's a doll! The prettiest one I ever saw in my life. Do look!'

But Jonathan was picking up a train and a big ship with magnificent sails and three teddy bears in a row together! Elizabeth began to pick up things too. Another doll, two fat toy pandas, a doll's house with its chimney off, a musical box. Really there seemed to be no end to the toys in their garden that night!

The children piled them all together and went through them again. What a wonderful collection! Elizabeth nursed each of the dolls, and Jonathan wound up the train to see if the clockwork was still all right.

'*Where* did they come from? Did that aeroplane really drop them?' said Elizabeth.

'No, I don't think so,' said Jonathan. 'You know, Elizabeth, I think Santa Claus must have galloped over here and he's dropped his sack of toys. Look up on the roof. That looks like a big, burst-open sack there, doesn't it?'

It did. The children stared at it. 'Well – I suppose we can't keep any of these lovely things then,' said

Elizabeth with a sigh. 'I do love this baby doll so much. What shall we do with everything?'

'I expect when Santa Claus misses his sack, he will come back and look for it,' said Jonathan. 'We had better put everything into one of our own sacks – there are plenty in the shed. We will leave it standing in the garden for him to see. He will easily spot it in the moonlight.'

'I wish we could keep just one thing each,' said Elizabeth.

'Well, we can't,' said Jonathan. 'For one thing the toys aren't ours. And for another thing you know jolly well we don't deserve anything.'

They found a big sack and put everything into it. Just as they were tying up the neck, they heard the sound of bells again – and there, up in the bright moonlit sky, they saw the reindeer sleigh, and Santa Claus leaning over, looking downwards. He saw the children, of course, and down he came, the reindeer landing softly in the garden snow.

'Your sack fell on our roof!' said Jonathan, running

up to help him out of the sleigh. 'We've collected all the toys, sir, and put them into another sack. Here they are!'

'What good, honest children!' beamed Santa Claus, taking the big sack from them. 'I'm sure I must have your names down on my list. I'll let you *choose* your Christmas toys, for being such a help. Let me see, what *are* your names?'

'Elizabeth and Jonathan, Santa Claus,' said Elizabeth.

Santa Claus at once looked solemn. 'Oh! I'm sorry – your names are *not* down on my list for presents this year. Bad work at school – and rudeness to your mother. What a pity!'

The children went red. 'Yes,' said Jonathan. 'It's more than a pity, Santa Claus. Our mother's ill and in hospital, and we can't forgive ourselves for making her unhappy. And our father has just had our bad reports when he's feeling miserable about Mother. I can tell you we're going to turn over a new leaf next year!'

'Yes, we're both going to be top of our forms, and we're going to make such a fuss of Mother when she comes home that she will be happier than she's ever been before!' said Elizabeth. 'We didn't expect any presents from you this year. We haven't even hung our stockings up.'

'Well – it's good to see children who are not ashamed to own up when they've done wrong,' said Santa Claus. 'I think I'd better leave you two little things, just as a reward for picking up all my toys for me.'

'We'd rather you left Mother something at the hospital,' said Jonathan. 'She broke her watch the day before she was ill. Could you leave her a new one, do you think?'

'Oh yes!' said Santa Claus. 'I'll do that. Goodbye and thank you – and just see that I have your names down on my list for *next* Christmas!'

He drove off into the air with a jingling of bells, and the children went to bed, feeling sleepy. They were fast asleep in two minutes.

In the morning, what a surprise! Standing at the end of Elizabeth's bed was the big baby doll she had picked up the night before – and at the end of Jonathan's was the toy train!

'He came back! Oh, he's the kindest old fellow in the world!' cried Elizabeth. 'Jonathan, I do hope he remembered Mother's watch.'

He did, of course. She was even more surprised than the children to find such a lovely present by her bedside – and one that nobody knew anything about at all!

'Well, that was an adventure that did a lot of good!' said Santa Claus, as he galloped back to Toyland that night. 'It's nice to meet children who know how to turn over a new leaf. What a surprise they'll get on Christmas morning! I wonder if their names will be down on my list for next Christmas.'

Of course they will, Santa Claus! We can all tell you that for certain!

The Little
Reindeer Bell

The Little
Reindeer Bell

NOW IT HAPPENED one year that Santa Claus had to put a new reindeer with the others in his sleigh, because one of his old ones had a dreadful cough.

'I'll have to have someone in place of you, Quickfoot,' said Santa Claus. 'You'd wake up all the children on Christmas Eve by coughing on the roofs of their houses. I never heard such a cough in my life. Go to your stable and keep warm.'

'Sir, I think young Quick-as-the-Wind would do well,' said the stable man. 'He's a young reindeer, but very sensible, and I think he could soon learn to gallop through the sky.'

'Right,' said Santa Claus, 'I'll give him a trial run with the others, a week before Christmas. Have my sleigh ready, and a sack of potatoes in it, instead of a sack of toys – just so that we have plenty of weight to pull.'

Well, on the Saturday before Christmas, the reindeer were harnessed to the sleigh. The new one, Quick-as-the-Wind, was very excited and proud. He kept tossing his head in delight, and his bells jingled loudly.

'Do keep still,' said the stable man. 'And don't toss your head when you're in the sky – you might tear a cloud to pieces!'

'I hope there won't *be* any clouds in the sky,' said Santa Claus. 'If they're thick they may make me lose my way. Now then – are we ready? All you have to do, Quick-as-the-Wind, is to gallop in exact time with the others, and don't get out of step. Geeeeeee-UP!'

And away they went, galloping straight up in the sky, and then across it at top speed. It was a bright, starry night, but there was no moon. Quick-as-the-Wind was enjoying himself very much – how wonderful it was to gallop through the air! He threw up his head in delight, and all the bells on his antlers jingled loudly.

He tossed his head in joy again and again, and one of the bells became loose. At the next toss of his head the bell was jerked right off, and fell down, down, down through the air to the earth below. None of the reindeer knew it had gone, and Santa Claus didn't guess either.

Now, far down below, three children were looking out of their window before going to bed. Peter, who had ears as sharp as a dog, heard bells jingling quite clearly on the frosty air.

'Listen! Bells!' he said. 'It might be Christmas Eve, with Santa Claus galloping through the sky and reindeer bells jingling merrily.'

'Well, it *isn't* Christmas Eve!' said Dilys, looking up into the starry sky. Then she suddenly cried out in surprise and pointed upwards. 'Look – what's that passing across the sky – see, up there!'

The others looked intently, and sure enough they could *just* make out something passing swiftly across the stars! Was it an aeroplane? No, a plane would make a noise – and the only noise they could hear was the far-off sound of jingling!

'Strange!' said Thomas. 'Very strange. Whatever can it be?'

And then, just at that moment a little shining object fell into their garden. It didn't shine very brightly, but just caught the lamplight from their window as it fell. The children heard a tiny thud, a little jingle, and then all was quiet.

'What was that?' said Peter, startled. 'Did you see something fall? I heard a little thud too.'

'Yes. Let's go and see what it was,' said Dilys, suddenly excited. 'I say – could it have fallen from that thing we saw in the sky?'

'Well – I suppose it might have,' said Thomas, scrambling down from the window seat. 'Let's go and look for it!'

All three ran downstairs and into the garden. Peter took his torch with him and it wasn't long before they found the fallen reindeer bell. It was quite big, beautifully polished, and jingled loudly when Peter shook it.

'What a big bell!' he said. 'It's as big as our ping-pong ball. Wherever did it come from? No aeroplane would carry *bells*!'

'Let's go and show it to Mother,' said Dilys. So they went indoors and found their mother. 'Look,' said Dilys, 'this fell into our garden just now, Mother. A bell!'

'What a strange thing to happen!' said their mother, handling it. 'And see – it's got letters engraved on it!'

'Yes – two beautifully engraved letters,' said Peter. 'Look – that's an S. And this one's a C. Goodness – S.C.! I suppose they are the initials of the owner of the bell. It must be a very *important* bell.'

'S.C.,' said Thomas slowly. 'My word – I wonder – no that's silly! It couldn't be!'

'*What* do you wonder?' asked Peter.

'Well – S.C. might stand for Santa Claus,' said Thomas. 'Mightn't it?'

The others stared at him, full of sudden excitement. 'That thing we saw jingling through the sky – it might have been a sleigh!' cried Dilys.

'But Santa Claus only rides out on Christmas Eve,' said Thomas.

'How do *you* know? He might take his reindeer for a run any time – he might want to make sure they knew their way for Christmas time!' said Dilys. 'Oh, I'm absolutely *certain* it was Santa Claus and his reindeer! And one of the reindeer bells came loose and dropped off – into our garden!'

'Oh, darling – I don't really think such a thing could happen!' said her mother, laughing. 'Though it certainly is strange that the bell has those initials on it.'

'Mother – it must be a very *lucky* bell if it belongs to Santa Claus,' said Peter. 'Perhaps it will bring us good luck. Oh, I wish Daddy was here too, to hear about this. He won't be home for Christmas, will he?'

'I'm afraid not,' said his mother. 'He's a thousand miles away! We'll have to manage without him this Christmas.'

Dilys took the bell into her hand and warmed it. 'Bell – you must be very, very lucky,' she said. 'Bring us luck this week, please. Let's have lots of lovely presents for Christmas! Do try and be lucky, bell!'

'What are we going to do with it?' asked Peter. 'We ought to try to find the owner, if it isn't Santa Claus.'

'It's his bell, I'm sure it is!' said Dilys. 'It *must* have fallen off one of his galloping reindeer!'

'Well – we could always put it up on the roof, lit by a little lamp!' said Thomas with a laugh. 'Then if he comes to *our* house on Christmas Eve, he'll be sure to see it and take it away!'

'Oh, yes – let's do that when Christmas comes!' said Dilys. 'We'll know Santa Claus has been, if the bell is gone!'

The children put the bell in the middle of the sitting room mantelpiece, and looked at it a dozen times a day.

Dilys kept rubbing it and wishing with it. She said that she was so sure it was a lucky bell that she wanted to make the most of it every minute she could!

But somehow that bell *didn't* bring them luck! In fact, a lot of horrid things happened that week. First of all the presents sent to them for Christmas by their father didn't arrive. 'They must have been lost on the way,' said Mother. 'They should have been here by now.'

And then Mother had a *big* piece of bad luck! She lost her purse! She took it out shopping with her to buy a big chicken for Christmas Day, a Christmas tree, lots of presents, and other things. She had pushed her bag into her shopping basket – and then when she put down her hand for it – it was gone!

'Somebody must have taken it!' said Mother in a panic. 'Oh, and I had such a lot of money in it! Peter, Dilys, Thomas – it was our Christmas money. Now we shan't be able to have half the things I wanted you to have!'

'Poor Mother!' said Thomas. 'I'll go to the police station and report it. Perhaps it dropped out of your basket. If so, someone may bring it back.'

But nobody did. It had been stolen. What bad luck, just in Christmas week! The children were very sad because they had so much looked forward to a good time at Christmas – but they were so sorry for their mother that they didn't make any fuss at all!

Then Dilys caught a dreadful cold and had to go to bed. She scowled at the bell as she went upstairs. 'Horrid bell! Unlucky bell! Nothing has gone right since we found it. For goodness' sake let's get rid of it, Thomas. Be sure to put it up on the roof so that Santa Claus can take the horrid thing away!'

Well, on Christmas Eve when Santa Claus went out in his sleigh, he was indeed astonished to see his lost reindeer bell gleaming in the light of a little lamp, up on the roof of the children's house! Thomas had gone up to the loft, opened the skylight there, and put out the bell and the lamp. There they were, waiting for Santa Claus, at about half past eleven on Christmas Eve!

'Well! If that isn't the bell Quick-as-the-Wind lost last week!' said Santa Claus. 'Now who found it – and how kind to put it up here for me to take! I've a good mind to knock at the front door and find out if the children's parents are still up. I see there is a light downstairs.'

The children's mother was most astonished to hear someone knocking at the front door. A voice said, 'Don't be alarmed. It's only Santa Claus. I've just found my reindeer bell on the roof.'

'Oh! Do come in!' called the mother, and opened the door to Santa Claus. 'I'm still busy trying to finish some little presents for the children,' she said. 'We had some bad luck this week and lost our Christmas money. The children hoped that your reindeer bell might be a lucky one – but it wasn't!'

'Hmm!' said Santa Claus. 'I'm sorry about that. Our bells are neither lucky *nor* unlucky – just bells. But maybe *I'm* a bit lucky! What were you going to buy with the money you lost?'

'Oh – the usual things,' said the mother. 'A good plump bird, a Christmas cake, decorations and chocolates and sweets and fruit – and presents, of course!'

'You leave all that to me, and get to bed,' said Santa Claus kindly. 'You look tired out. Where's your husband? Can't he help?'

'He's a thousand miles away!' said the mother with a sigh. 'Oh dear – you *are* kind – and I haven't even offered you anything to eat or drink. Are you cold – would you like some cocoa or hot milk?'

'No thank you,' said Santa Claus. 'I would *like* to say yes – but this is my busy night, you know. Now – will you please leave all this work you're doing, and go to bed? I've something to do here that I don't want you to see. Goodnight – and a very happy Christmas!'

The mother went upstairs in a daze. Could it *really* be true that Santa Claus himself had come knocking at the door so late at night? And he had actually found that bell up on the roof! How wonderful!

Santa Claus became very busy when the mother had gone. Strange noises came from the sitting room and the kitchen. One of the noises was made by Santa Claus – he hummed quietly to himself because he was feeling very pleased. How pleasant to bring a little good luck to such a nice family!

The reindeer waiting outside couldn't *imagine* why he was so long. They stamped their hooves, and jingled their bells impatiently. It was a wonder that the sleeping children didn't hear them!

Santa Claus came out at last, very hot, very happy and in a great hurry. He clambered into his sleigh and shook the reins. 'Make haste now!' he said. 'We've lost a lot of time – you must gallop twice as fast as usual!' And away they went, jingling through the sky!

The children awoke about seven o'clock next morning. It was Peter who saw the wonderful sight first. He gave a loud shout. 'Dilys! Thomas! Look at all this!'

What a marvellous sight they saw! Toys of all kinds were piled here and there – their stockings were full to the top – and in a separate corner, on an armchair, was a pile of things marked '*For your mother*'.

'A woolly coat, stockings, a new electric kettle, a box of chocolates – I say, look at all these lovely things for Mother. Whatever does it all mean?' cried Dilys. 'Mother, Mother, come here!'

'Oh!' said Mother, coming quickly into the bedroom.

'*Oh!* Good gracious! So this is what Santa Claus was busy about after I went to bed!'

'Santa Claus! What do you mean, Mother? Did he come? Did he find the bell? Mother, what's it all about?' cried Peter.

'I'll just go and light the fire downstairs, then I'll tell you all about it!' said Mother – but no sooner was she downstairs than she called back in excitement. 'Come down here – just come down here!'

Down rushed the three children – and stared in amazement at the sitting room. It was beautifully decorated – and in the corner was a lovely Christmas tree, hung with ornaments and parcels. Tins of biscuits and boxes of chocolates, and all kinds of fruit were on the sideboard – and in the larder was a fine turkey, ready to roast, and all kinds of goodies.

'Did – did Santa Claus do all this?' asked Peter in wonder. 'Why? I don't understand it. How did he know we hadn't much for Christmas?'

'I'll tell you,' said his mother, and soon they had all heard how Santa Claus had come knocking at the door the night before, after he had found his reindeer bell on the roof.

'I *wish* I'd seen him, Mother!' said Dilys longingly. '*Why* didn't you wake us? If only I'd heard him knock-knock-knocking . . .'

Knock, knock, knock! Was that Santa Claus at the door again? Someone was there, knocking loudly. It must be old Santa Claus! Now they could thank him!

But it wasn't Santa Claus – it was their father! There he was, beaming at them. 'I got sudden leave and flew home!' he said. 'And a funny journey it was too – I thought I heard jingling bells all the way!'

Jingling bells! Now what was the meaning of *that*? But there was no time to explain anything, everyone wanted to hug and be hugged. And who minded if Daddy hadn't had time to bring them any special presents?

'*You're* our best Christmas present!' cried Dilys. 'Oh, why did we say that bell was unlucky? It was the luckiest find we *ever*, *ever* had!'

Acknowledgements

All efforts have been made to seek necessary permissions. The stories in this publication first appeared in the following publications:

'The Christmas Present' first appeared in *Hello Twins, Little Book No. 4*, published by Brockhampton Press in 1951.

'The Midnight Goblins' first appeared in *Sunny Stories for Little Folks*, No. 21, 1927.

'The Christmas Tree Fairy' first appeared in *Enid Blyton's Sunny Stories*, No. 46, 1937.

The extract from 'What They Did at Miss Brown's School' was published as part of *Enid Blyton's Book of the Year* by Evans Brothers in 1941.

'The Stolen Reindeer' first appeared in *The Teachers World*, No. 931, 1922.

'The Vanishing Nuts' first appeared in *Sunny Stories for Little Folks*, No. 89, 1930.

'The Christmas Tree Aeroplane' first appeared in *Enid Blyton's Sunny Stories*, No. 153, 1939.

'A Christmas Story' first appeared in *The Teachers World*, No. 1595, 1933.

'The Little Fairy Doll' first appeared in *The Teachers World*, No. 1491, 1931.

'The Very Lovely Pattern' first appeared in *The Enid Blyton Nature Readers*, No. 29, published by Macmillan in 1946.

'The Cold Snowman' first appeared as 'The Cold Snow-Man' in *Sunny Stories for Little Folks*, No. 200, 1934.

'The Lucky Number' first appeared in *Tiny Tots*, published by Cassell in 1925.

'The Little Fir Tree' first appeared as 'The Little Fir-Tree' in *The Enid Blyton Nature Readers*, No. 30, published by Macmillan in 1946.

'Bobbo's Magic Stocking' first appeared in *Sunny Stories for Little Folks*, No. 35, 1927.

'The Big Girl's Balloon' first appeared in *Enid Blyton's Sunny Stories*, No. 368, 1945.

'Amelia Jane and the Snow' first appeared in *Enid Blyton's Sunny Stories*, No. 105, 1939.

'The Very Full Stocking' first appeared as 'The Very-Full Stocking' in *Enid Blyton's Sunny Stories*, No. 206, 1940.

'A Week Before Christmas' first appeared in *Enid Blyton's Treasury*, published by the Evans Brothers in 1947.

'The Cracker Fairies' first appeared as 'The Cracker-Fairies' in *Enid Blyton's Sunny Stories*, No. 153, 1939.

'The Dog That Hated Christmas' first appeared in *Enid Blyton's Sunny Stories*, No. 101, 1938.

'The Goblin Who Stole Sweets' first appeared in *Enid Blyton's Sunny Stories*, No. 108, 1939.

'The Christmas Tree Party' first appeared as 'The Christmas-Tree Party' in *Enid Blyton's Sunny Stories*, No. 50, 1937.

'The Little Christmas Tree' first appeared in *The Teachers World*, No. 1699, 1935.

'What Happened on Christmas Eve' first appeared in *The Eighth Holiday Book*, published by Sampson Low in 1953.

'The Little Reindeer Bell' first appeared in *Enid Blyton's Magazine*, No. 24 Vol. 4, 1956.